News Anchor Sweetheart

*The girl has it all.
What can possibly go wrong?*

*"Engelhard zeroes in on a news anchor
who resembles Megyn Kelly.
It's fiction, but WOW!"*

by

JACK ENGELHARD

DayRay Literary Press
British Columbia, Canada

News Anchor Sweetheart

Copyright ©2016 by Jack Engelhard
ISBN-13 978-1-77143-277-1
First Edition

Library and Archives Canada Cataloguing in Publication
Engelhard, Jack, 1940-, author
News anchor sweetheart / by Jack Engelhard. -- First edition.
Issued in print and electronic formats.
ISBN 978-1-77143-276-4 (hbk.).--ISBN 978-1-77143-277-1 (pbk).--
ISBN 978-1-77143-278-8 (pdf)
Additional cataloguing data available from Library and Archives Canada

Jack Engelhard may be contacted through: **www.jackengelhard.com**

Cover artwork: Close-up of zipper © Violin | CanStockPhoto.com

Disclaimer: This is a work of fiction. The characters, names, incidents, organizations, businesses and dialogues are products of the author's imagination and are not to be construed as real. Any resemblance to actual events or persons living or dead is entirely coincidental.

All rights reserved. No part of this publication may be reproduced, stored in a retrieval system or transmitted in any form or by any means, electronic, mechanical, photocopying, recording or otherwise without the express written permission of the publisher, except in the case of brief and accurately credited quotations embodied in critical articles or reviews.

DayRay Literary Press is a literary imprint
of CCB Publishing: www.ccbpublishing.com

DayRay Literary Press
British Columbia, Canada
www.dayraypress.com

**International Bestselling Novelist Jack Engelhard
Author of *Indecent Proposal***

Translated into more than 22 languages and turned into a Paramount motion picture of the same name starring Robert Redford and Demi Moore.

News Anchor
Sweetheart

Great stuff from a great American novelist. Jack Engelhard (*Indecent Proposal... The Bathsheba Deadline... The Days of the Bitter End...*) brings it as only he can in language that is economical, hard-boiled and fast-paced to uncover through the art of fiction the naked truth about a TV news personality who resembles someone we all know.

Brilliant and elegantly done, Engelhard dishes the scoop on this "queen of Chick Power with legs to die for." What's it like to live under the glare of the spotlight, and to love after the lights go down?

In Engelhard's masterful rendering, we follow the glamorous Marjorie Carmen's rise to TV news stardom and what it took to get there, and what it takes to stay there. She came along when network TV news was dominated by living but dull white males. We root for her, hurt for her, love with her, find fault with her, and are always fascinated by her. But she is only half the story.

As she keeps winning, her husband, Rick, keeps losing. He's a failure. He must do something to prove he's worth keeping. The choice he makes leads to a fascinating result, and in taking us inside a teetering marriage, Engelhard is peerless. Watch for the third major character Engelhard adds to the picture – Ruben Franklin! This is a newsroom swashbuckler you'll never forget, just as you will never forget Marjorie Carmen, so fictitious, but so true. To know her, is to know our culture.

This is a superb, thrilling novel that must be read.

Praise received

"Engelhard zeroes in on a news anchor who resembles Megyn Kelly. It's fiction, but WOW!"
- Bonnie Kaye, author of *Jennifer Needle in Her Arm*

"Jack Engelhard's novels are filled to the brim with clear spirit, serious soul, and gritty honesty. His writing style is so light and bright it carries the reading in an effortless flow."
- Linda Shelnutt, author; most recent book,
  Myrtle's Penultimate Walkabout

"Engelhard writes with the sparseness of Hemingway and the moral intensity of I.B. Singer."
- Michael Foster, author of *Three in Love* (HarperCollins)

"Jack Engelhard is a writer without peer and the conscience of us all."
- John W. Cassell, author of *Crossroads: 1969*

Also by Jack Engelhard

Indecent Proposal: Fiction.
Translated into more than 22 languages and turned into a Paramount motion picture of the same name starring Robert Redford and Demi Moore.

Compulsive: A Novel: Fiction.

Escape From Mount Moriah: Memoir.
Award-winner for writing and film.

The Days of the Bitter End: Fiction.

Slot Attendant: A Novel About A Novelist: Fiction.

The Prince of Dice: Fiction.

The Bathsheba Deadline: Fiction.

The Girls of Cincinnati: Fiction

The Horsemen: Non-fiction.
Excerpted in *The New York Times*

* * * * *

A new Spanish language edition of *Indecent Proposal* was recently released in both print and e-book editions and made available for purchase worldwide.

The author wishes to express his gratitude and thanks to translators Frederick Martin-Del-Campo and Laura Mitre for their fine work in this and other projects.

More praise received for Jack Engelhard's books:

"Precise, almost clinical language…Is this book fun to read? You betcha."
- *The New York Times,* for *Indecent Proposal*

"Well-wrought characters, exhilarating pace…funny and gruff…a fast and well-crafted book."
- *Philadelphia Inquirer,* for *Indecent Proposal*

"*Compulsive* is enormously enjoyable, and so easy to get into."
- Kenneth Slawenski, (Random House) bestselling author of *J.D. Salinger: A Life* - www.deadcaulfields.com

"A towering literary achievement."
- Letha Hadady, author, for *The Bathsheba Deadline*

"Savor it…it may be the best, sharpest, most vivid portrait of life around the racetrack ever written."
- Ray Kerrison, *New York Post* columnist
writing for the *National Star,* for *The Horsemen*

"The refugee stories Engelhard preserves are boyhood memories of an almost Tom Sawyer character… adventurous, humorous, sometimes wonderfully strange."
- Chris Leppek, *Jewish News (Denver),*
for *Escape from Mount Moriah*

"What a great story. If you missed the 60s – if you missed the excitement, the passion, the radicalism, the thrills, the hopes and dreams – this book brings it all alive. I could not put it down."
- Kmgroup review, for *The Days of the Bitter End*

Dedicated to
Leslie, David, Rachel, Sarah, Toni...and Siena and Sofia!

...and to the loving memory of my parents
Noah and Ida

Immeasurable gratitude to
Jeffrey Farkas

Chapter 1

She was driving too fast and it was dark and the road was wet. He had been telling her to slow down but they had been arguing about everything else besides. This was just another dispute. There was nothing he could do to stop her, not now, not ever. She made a quick left to avoid oncoming headlights and wheeled them tumbling into a ditch.

"Are you okay?" she asked.

"I don't know," he said. "You?"

"I'm not sure," she said.

But she was able to move. She had bumped her skull and she was dizzy but maybe, she thought, this was the worst.

Fortunately, for her, she'd have another week to heal. The show, her show must go on. The ratings dropped something awful when for one reason or another she took off and someone had to sub her prime time hour. Russ Appleton hated to replace her even when her days off were legitimate.

Nobody did it like Marjorie Carmen. He'd nurtured her along gradually and carefully and systematically until he had her topping his network empire. This had been an entirely professional process. First a morning hour that he had her share with Bob Lyman. When the ratings proved her ready, he gave her an afternoon slot all to herself. Finally when the afternoon numbers zoomed, he gave her the night and stardom. She was tops. Her only rival with any chance of overtaking her was Megyn Kelly over at Fox.

At first Marjorie was truly grateful. She'd taken Communications at Temple and had expected nothing more than a spot on the local news even though on looks alone she knew she was national and world class. On smarts, too. So she'd been genuinely grateful for every favor and for every step upwards, but now she was grateful only as part of a performance.

She'd learned how to act, how to make journalism and acting work together. She could be sweet. She could be tough. She was always beautiful.

Rick, her husband, was a writer, a novelist. He used his given name, Rick Callow to maintain his honor, his dignity, his self-respect when he'd be far more successful cashing in as Mr. Marjorie Carmen, which he'd never do, most probably. His books were failing, and now his right ankle was twisted, stuck beneath a collapsing dashboard, and appeared broken. This became apparent and serious when he found himself unable to move and in terrible pain.

She'd have to take charge. Yes, the worst of it for her was a blow to the skull.

"The kids," she said, alarmed.

But Rick didn't answer. They were with her mother. She thought to call there first to assure everyone that she was all right. About Rick there'd be more explaining. About Rick it was always complicated or perhaps too simple, always. She came to her senses and called 9-1-1.

Location? No. She did not know where she was but they tracked her down and told her it would be awhile in this weather and so many accidents.

She gave her name. That always sped things up.

"We'll do what we can."

She was surprised. She was annoyed at the lack of excitement at the mention of her name. In the newsroom it was so different.

* * * * *

She reached Laurie in the newsroom. Laurie Pilgrim was managing editor.

"Oh my gawd!"

"It's not that bad," Marjorie explained. "Could have been much worse."

"Anything we can do?"

"No, we just have to wait."

"Oh my gawd!"

Marjorie got her off the phone quickly. She did not need hysterics at this time, only to think clearly and be brave, as brave as she'd been all her life. She'd been through much worse, including a helicopter crash in Afghanistan. So this really was not all that bad. The publicity would be bad. She had been drinking.

Well, she was not perfect. Never pretended to be. Her fans, her viewers, 12 million of them, sometimes 20 million of them, would have to take her as she was, warts and all. Besides, nobody else got hurt. She was bruised up and Rick of course...well Rick got the worst of it as he usually did these days and he had been drinking for all the reasons going back to his sense of failure.

He was roaring drunk at the party, which was why she took the wheel for a trip to settle it with his ex-wife who was demanding more alimony on the assumption that he was raking it in, which he was, but not on his own account. The money coming in, $25 million a year, came from Marjorie. But he was working on his next novel and this one, finally, was sure to be big. This one would show them all. This one would even the score. This one would win back Marjorie.

On that day she'd respect him again, admire him again, love him again. She never stopped loving him. Or so she kept saying.

She called him her "big bad hunk" and he was good looking. They made quite a couple. She still called him that but not as often.

Five years earlier it had been love at first sight. It was to be a second marriage for the both of them once the divorces came through and for her, for Marjorie, her divorce could not come soon enough. She was wild for Rick, who was still not a writer, but a lawyer who failed to make the cut at the firm, that came later, the writing, and she could not keep her hands off him, off Rick, he was so gorgeous.

They had fooled around well before they got married. They had to keep it quiet because of her career. The sex was great.

Not so much anymore and Rick wondered about this, about someone else having great sex with her.

* * * * *

Russ Appleton, her boss, the man who ran the network, the man who invented the network, reached her to say, "What the bloody hell!"

She explained. She was okay, considering, but Rick was suffering.

Russ had already contacted his own security people but there was nothing they could do. The network's choppers were down because of the weather and as for the cops, the cops and her alcohol level, that was the last thing anybody wanted. He ran a clean house. Even the hint of something scandalous could bring it all down, everything he had done to build it up from scratch.

"You can't stay in that car," he said.

In fact she could get out and reach the highway and hail a passing motorist. But then she'd have to leave Rick until an ambulance arrived.

"I'll do what I can," she told Russ.

"You better do more than that," Russ said hanging up.

He was angry. Well of course he was angry. His flare-ups frightened her. In this business nothing was certain and no reporter or anchor had it made. A bad night on the air, a dip in the ratings for whatever reason could spell doom. You were being judged from one broadcast to the next and the entire country sat as your jury.

You lived and breathed at the mercy of a point up or down in the ratings.

There was never a moment to call yourself a success when every night was opening night. You had to keep proving yourself.

You had to be smarter than every guest. You had to know everything. You had to keep up. No, you had to keep ahead.

She'd manage this.

Russ Appleton would not be that easy. He demanded creative perfection and spotless behavior. He was the law and he was the last of a kind, a broadcast whiz, a genius. While others were still anchoring dull white males, Russ Appleton built the network through Chick Power. He'd stacked the house with brainy blondes, all of them graduates from the finest schools with the finest legs, and nobody had legs like Marjorie Carmen had legs.

"Rick?" she said.

She had no tolerance for pain or rather she refused to accept it for herself. She'd play pretend. She'd always done so in the past. Two miscarriages. She did so again. Nothing happened, she told herself.

Nothing really. Nothing really that bad. This could be fixed. This will be fixed.

"Rick?"

He was conscious but suffering. That was the part about him she found most difficult, the suffering, the suffering in silence, his pride and his nobility in suffering, his *go on don't worry about me* performances that she found so unmanly about him and so displeasing.

He was still a good man, though. He worked hard at the new profession he had carved out for himself, the writing, and he was okay with the kids. She had no complaints. She kept rooting for him, cheering him on and admiring him for his tenacity.

One bestseller could turn everything around. She wanted this. She wanted his fame, his money, his glory to make him her equal.

She had never meant to rise so far above him. She wanted both of them to shine together, as a team, as a family. But fate chose her.

"Rick?"

He was fading. But she had stopped the bleeding from his ankle.

"I may have to go," she told him as she mopped his brow from torrents of perspiration.

She needed to tell him that she'd have to leave, leave him alone until help arrived. She was not abandoning him. Of course not. One of them had to do something and as luck would have it she was the only one capable. She needed to be sure he understood.

He nodded, or appeared to understand.

* * * * *

But stepping out was not so simple. The door was jammed and the soil was deep in mud. She heard sirens and changed her mind. They might be coming. She tried 9-1-1 again and again was told to sit tight. An ambulance was on its way. When? This, nobody could say. There'd been so many accidents, so many calls, most of them ahead of hers. She'd have to wait her turn.

"Wait my turn?"

That's what she'd done all her life, thank you very much. So? What? Was she about to start an argument with an emergency operator?

But she sure had a new feature to add to her lineup. Another thing wrong with this country. Well, come to think of it, her nightly show was all about that, that and practically nothing else. This came to her as something of a revelation. Yes, only bad news is news.

The people who came on had nothing but complaints, most especially on politics. She tried to stay neutral. But gradually she'd begun turning to the Right. Or, others said, gradually she'd begun turning to the Left. So she made no one happy except that she was beautiful and had a way with people on either side.

There was no doubting her charm when she meant to be charming or her mockery when she meant to cut.

The camera loved her and made love to her and for all that she had learned something unique from an actor whose lesson was to always treat your audience as one person, one person in your living room, never as a crowd, and to win this friend with a single thought, "I want to fuck you."

* * * * *

"Rick," she said, "I'm not sure what to do."
She was not playing this part to man him out of his misery. She truly did not know what to do.
If she stays and waits it out, who knows, and if she goes, same question.
"Go," he said. "I think you should go."
She thought about this for some time, time enough, she hoped, for someone to show up and spare her the decision.
"Will you be all right?" she asked, knowing immediately that it was a stupid question.
The pain, he realized, wasn't all that bad, not as bad as it had been at first. This could be a good sign or a very bad sign.
"I'm always all right," he snapped. "I'm always good enough. Isn't that how it works with us?"
So there it was, she thought.
"Rick, please."
"Don't mind me," he said. "I'm just out of my head."

He had already downed an overdose of the aspirin that they always brought along and he wanted two more.

"That could be dangerous. You know what it does..."

"Please don't tell me what it does. I know what it does."

"There's no need," she began...

"That's right. There's no need for anything."

"This is no time to argue," she said.

True, he thought, because she wins anyway. She was the winner in the family and he hated himself for resenting that fact.

She had done nothing, ever, to lord it over him. She deserved better than his resentments and she deserved better than his failures.

Timing, only the timing was wrong. He had caught her just when she was going up and she got trapped with him just when he was going down. So much of it was luck. They had each put in the same amount of hard work but even between twins usually one rises as the other one falls.

In a marriage it must be the same deal.

Only seldom does life make a fair bargain.

* * * * *

"I think you should run along," he said.
"I don't care for the language of that," she said.
"Really, I mean it," he insisted.
"Really?"

"Really," he said.

"You're sounding bitter."

Probably, he thought. Bitterness had never been his style but damn it was hurtful being second best, an also-ran, a tag-along. Even now and especially now he was thinking about his novel, the work still to be done to make it perfect for himself and presentable to the publisher, who was already on board with a guarantee, due mainly, or exclusively to her name, not his.

But the novel was his. There wasn't much more to do. He had a hundred pages more to go, as he had it figured. Or maybe 50. How did it go? Write your heart out, take a nap, and then cut it in half. So it was nearly done and then what? Fame? Glory? If there was a God in heaven, yes.

He really did want her to go. He never could write when she was around. The laptop was there in the back seat. Maybe he could write through the pain.

When she was around he felt himself being mocked. So he couldn't write as he normally would.

No, it always came out wrong, forced, when she was in the house, which was seldom, true.

He'd taken that night class on creative writing at Columbia even though he knew that writing can't be taught. It's there or it's not. With discipline, with effort, with sweat, sometimes people with half a talent can write one, if only one good book. James Jones did it with *From Here to Eternity*.

He'd been embarrassed to tell Marjorie the class he'd been taking. He told her it was something on tax law he was reviewing and brushing up on.

But Marjorie knew and rather than scoff, no rather than that, she was proud of him. That was a winning move whether it succeeded or not.

He'd written two other novels. Both succeeded at first when readers found out who he was, or rather whom he was married to, and when that wore off, the books flopped. He couldn't figure out what had happened and neither could Marjorie. The books were good or at least as good as anything else on the market.

So next time, this time, he'd have to do better, or maybe worse, because some very bad books were selling very well and so much of it depended on the friends you had in the reviewer trade, meaning *The New York Times* and *The New York Review of Books* along with *The New Yorker*.

That was a different crowd. Even Marjorie didn't belong. No, that was altogether different.

There was no secret handshake to get in. Or maybe there was. Hell, maybe there was.

No, he'd never set out to write a bad book. Nobody did. From page one everyone left the gate evenly for the finish line, a masterpiece.

Could this one be the one?

"I do think you should go," he told her.

Chapter 2

Marjorie was still unsure of what action to take and then Russ Appleton phoned to ask what's happening. He had calmed down, it seemed.

She explained the quandary she was in.

"Then go," he said. "You'd be doing it for his own good. Maybe you'd stop a medic on the road if he's in the shape you say he's in."

"It's bad."

"So what's stopping you?"

"It would seem like I'm deserting him."

"No, you'd be helping him."

"Just leave him like that?" she asked.

"Think of the big picture."

That was Russ all right. Think of the big picture.

"Help is bound to come," she said. "I'd rather be here when it comes."

"You mean the image of Marjorie Carmen abandoning her husband if word gets out?"

"I did not have that in mind," she huffed.

No, she didn't. She did not have that in mind. Or maybe she did. She wasn't sure.

"How badly are you cut?" Russ asked.

"Not too bad. Just a swelling on my forehead."
"Can make-up take care of it, you think?"
"Yes," she said.
"You were lucky."
"Yes," she agreed.
"You're due back in a few days, you know."
"Of course I know."
"Then you also know about the interview that came through while you were out?"
"Which one?" she asked.

There were always interviews being arranged whether she was in or out.

"The one with the President."
"Russ, you're kidding."
"It's set for two weeks from now. The word came through an hour ago. I didn't want to tell you in the condition you're in. You've got enough on your mind."

She let that sink in. This was the prize she'd been after for...well since she'd taken the top anchor spot, second only to Matt Owens.

"Of all the timing," she said.
"I know."

She had already nabbed kings, queens, princes, but never the President of the United States. He hated the network because the network hated him. This was the catch that would totally, finally and totally legitimize Alpha News, first in the ratings but last to be licensed.

"You have choices to make," Russ said, but she wasn't listening because of what happened in succession.

A tow truck pulled up way up on the edge of the highway and noting the mudslide the guy yelling down to Marjorie said that he'd need to call for further assistance. It was that bad, with the rain still coming down without letup. She had managed to step out of the car, step into the moving slush to tell the guy that she had a seriously injured man in the car.

That settled it and made it impractical because to move the car would jostle a man in such straits and could prove deadly.

No, medical help would have to come first, and it did. But this driver said that the slush being nearly a river, there was no way of reaching down by foot.

A tow truck would have to come first and now, for the first time, Marjorie Carmen, star news and opinion anchor for Alpha News, broke down in tears.

* * * * *

Later, much later, news reports would allege that Marjorie Carmen had been no help for a husband who needed help and comfort.

Nonsense, most likely.

So finally there were no choices to make.

"I'm going," she told Rick.

"Of course you are," he said. "Off you go."

There had been a phone call, a call she frequently got from news director Ruben Franklin. They worked closely together and the rumor was how close? For Rick, it was between close enough or too close. But Ruben Franklin was only one of several suspects so far as Rick was concerned.

There'd been late dinners and sudden meetings with a number of staffers and beyond that a word here and there about several members of Congress.

A woman with her looks, those legs, that power – anything was possible.

Ruben Franklin was something else. He'd come over from the big one in London. He'd been a reviewer of the Arts, primarily books and was an author himself, several times on the short list for the Man Booker Prize. He dated socialites and he romanced famous actresses. He was said to be irresistible to women and was famous for appearing in natty attire, a white shirt always wide open at the collar.

He came from awesome wealth. Never really had to work, but he did. He was so famous in England that his initials RF were enough.

Russ Appleton had nabbed him and brought him over to New York with freedoms to operate that he could not turn down. Money he did not need.

Ruben was a philosopher as well as a writer and broadcaster and he had phoned her to say that he had made his way over and was at the top of the cliff with the motor running. Somehow he'd beaten the many weather-related roadblocks from Manhattan to this Hicksville. He could not come down to fetch her up. The treacherous conditions would only sink them both.

One particular thought came to Rick instinctively – How perfect.

"It's the only way," Marjorie told Rick.

He didn't answer.

"Rick?"

"Why all this talk?" he snapped.

"You can't let yourself think what you're thinking," she cautioned.

"You don't know what I'm thinking."

"Good," she said. "You'll be all right. I'll bring back help the minute I grab somebody, anybody."

"Thanks."

"Are you in less pain?" she asked. "You seem to be in less pain."

"I'll be all right as soon as you leave. So will you, I imagine."

"Rick, please."

"Go."

She went.

Chapter 3

Marjorie Carmen managed to trudge up the slope, a hazardous trip until, drenched and a horror to behold, she reached Ruben's Mercedes. She got in and neither of them said a word for a while. She needed to collect her thoughts. He knew how it worked with her. He'd give her all the time she needed.

He'd already notified the police. But they'd told him that all things considered it may be up to three or four hours before they could get to Rick. These were unusual circumstances. The worst rainfall in over 40 years. Flooding everywhere. Every emergency vehicle was in use and behind schedule.

"How did you manage?" she finally got around to recover enough to ask.

Ruben Franklin always managed. He ran with the motto, "Anything is possible." He told her so.

"That can be taken two ways," she answered.

"Not with me."

She knew this. Not with him. Not with Ruben Franklin, the winner, a winner in a world of losers. Her husband and his broken toe came to mind.

More silence until finally he turned to her. "Where's the damage?"

"I only bumped my head," she said.

"Oh, that," he said. "Nothing much."

"Considering."

"Rick?"

"Yes, Rick."

"That bad?"

"Pretty bad."

"How's he managing?"

"Bitching."

"Got that, but I mean…"

"He's taken aspirin and tranquilizers. At best it's just a sprain. But he can't move. He mustn't be moved."

"How worried are you?"

"Plenty."

They were stopped by a State Police roadblock and were detoured to a side road.

"Well," he said, "the chances of making it to Manhattan or anywhere civilized are nil."

"How British," she said.

"I'm trying to learn your language."

She smiled.

He knew how to make her smile. He knew how to make her do practically anything. Between them hardly anything was out of bounds.

"There'll be none of that," she had told him with a wiggle and a flirtatious smile, back then, at the very beginning, when she'd found herself unbearably attracted to him. But there was, there was plenty of that and it could not be helped. During periods of guilt she resolved to make it stop, but to no avail.

Marjorie knew the risk, but she remained defiant. A touch of adultery, these days...so?

That was how Ruben put it when carrying the guilt got too heavy for Marjorie.

"We're only doing what comes naturally," he'd say to cover his own guilt. Or he'd say, "Marrying Rick, that had been the mistake. Not this. Not us."

Did he really believe that what they were doing was right? Sometimes he did. Sometimes he didn't. Raised in affluence, he knew that the usual rules seldom applied to the moneyed class. They had their own rules and were answerable only to their own kind.

"This rain," she said as Ruben kept to the flooded roads.

She texted Rick but he failed to respond. That could mean anything. She felt awful.

"What was the reason for this misbegotten trip?" Ruben asked.

"His ex."

"Oh. I see. She wants more money."

"Right."

"Your money, actually."

"Actually," she said, loving him for his Briticisms.

"There'll never be an end to this, you know."

"I'm glad you're saying this," she said.

"Why?"

"Because you're not the type to say everything will be all right when you know it won't."

"I do see trouble ahead."

Her salary kept making headlines and there was talk, chatter, buzz that unless she got more, she might leave the Alpha News network.

Everybody wanted her. She was "in the midst of renegotiations with Alpha News management."

Ruben was also not the type for accusations, condolences or regrets, and not once had he asked her how she had managed to blunder into such a marriage.

But it did seem, now as much as ever, that everything Rick touched, this husband of hers, went sour. Ruben meant to ask her – could this not have been resolved with a phone call? Was this some form of blackmail? If a trip was necessary, couldn't he have gone alone? Why did he need to schlep her along?

But he would not ask any of this, certainly not now. Later, perhaps, but not now.

Ruben had been astute to the comings and goings of that marriage between Marjorie Carmen and Rick Callow. He knew about the good times as well, when it had been all promise for him as much as for her. There'd been the best of years; the sharing between them, the planning, the dreaming and each had been dealt a hand above the deck.

Then, when his talent was unable to match his ambition, it all went to pot. He couldn't keep up. He was left standing as she kept rising higher and higher. Everything fell apart for him. But he kept on typing. He kept turning out pages lonely for approval.

Now Ruben himself was in a fix. This could lead to scandal, for the both of them, for the three of them, though for Rick the end could be an advantage.

Rick had nothing to lose, no job, no reputation. For himself, for Ruben, and for Marjorie, emphatically for Marjorie, there was everything to lose.

Ruben found himself getting angry. This man Rick, this husband of hers, was a loser and a putz. He was harmful and he was contagious.

"We'll make camp in there," he said, approaching the sign that read Motel.

"Whatever you say," she said.

She tried Rick again and again there was no response.

"We need to stop, regroup, and make plans, whatever plans there are to be made," Ruben said.

"Yes," Marjorie said. "Yes."

* * * * *

News reports and gossip would later assert that Marjorie Carmen had been thinking only of herself, that she had not tried hard enough to save her husband. She could have done more to pry him loose (when in fact that could have been an entirely dangerous attempt from a non-professional).

She should have stayed with him longer, they said. She should have done much more.

In fact she had managed to somehow reach the highway fighting against heavy rains and mudslides in an attempt to get help from any passing motorist, but no one stopped and she could hardly be seen in the downpour and within the blur of the fog.

She had risked her life for him. Some argued in her favor. Others did not.

* * * * *

Checking in would be difficult, but she was a wreck from all the rain, so she might not be recognized.

"Hey, you're somebody, right?" said the kid checking them in.

"I'm nobody," Ruben said, giving it a laugh.

"No, I mean her."

Ruben slipped him a hundred dollar bill. The kid turned it back.

"We don't run that kind of place," the kid said.

"Sorry," Ruben said. "My mistake."

"Goodnight," said the kid.

* * * * *

Marjorie ran straight for the shower and stayed there for quite some time. "What was that all about?" she asked when she got out.

"Nothing," Ruben said.

"You know it was something."

"Nothing really."

Ruben was on the phone to the network's security department for advice on what to do for Rick. Was a chopper really out of the question?

Yes. No chance.

He tried other numbers, other contacts with the same result. Nothing much to be done until the weather eases up.

People were dying out there; a broken ankle or whatever would have to wait. But the man is stuck in that car!

"We're doing what we can."

Of all the rotten luck, and now himself right in the middle. Well, he'd been through tight spots before, wars, tornadoes, hurricanes, but never a mudslide.

This was a mudslide, for Rick, for Marjorie, for Ruben, and for the entire Alpha News network, that's what this was, a mudslide. Sinking together.

So far, now thinking as a news director, he was satisfied that no one had gotten hurt, so far as publicity. We'll see how long this lasts.

The golden girl of network news must not be touched by this. Or else we all go down.

Amazing, he thought, how one man, one idiot, can bring catastrophe upon all our heads.

First, we nearly lose her through an accident that's really his fault. Next, we could lose her through the scandal of an anchorwoman screwing her news director, information readily in hand if anyone were to ask Greg Olman, who hosted the four o'clock hour and served as the newsroom snitch.

The clash between them, between Ruben Franklin and Greg Olman was immediate and lasting. Olman could slant the news with the arch of an eyebrow.

Well, so could Marjorie, but when she did it people smiled.

Olman had it in for Blacks and Jews but was subtle enough to push it through as a signal to his own kind. Ruben hated gossips and sneaks and when he ordered Olman to present his on-air copy for review and editing, that's when Olman began his gossip campaign against Ruben. Nothing big. Just wondering why Ruben and Marjorie take such long lunches together.

He could fire the son of a bitch. He should fire the son of a bitch. But there are contracts and there are unions.

In nothing but a towel covering her she sat down next to Ruben, placed her head on his shoulder and they sat there like that until he removed the towel.

Why, they agreed, should now be any different.

* * * * *

Later they turned on the TV and on Alpha News they were in time to catch anchor Greg Olman deliver the news that Marjorie Carmen will soon be ending her vacation and she's bound to be back as hot as ever – with a surprise interview. "So don't touch that dial, and if you're out there somewhere listening in, Marjorie, we miss you."

"Hot as ever, aye?"

"I really can't stand him," said Marjorie.

"He knows his stuff."

"He knows too much."

"I notice you two never talk."

"He's so... typical."

Marjorie fit in well. She got along with most of the reporters and anchors, even the women, though lately there had been some coolness.

"Do you ever get that?" she asked.

"You mean why her and not me? Yes."

"Really. They never say it to me."

"That's why I'm there, Marjorie. I'm your buffer."

She was silent for a while.

"Keep doing that," she said.

"Like that?"

"Yes. Yes. Yes."

* * * * *

Ruben placed a call to Greg Olman to tell him to knock it off.

"Yes, sir, but I don't know what you mean."

"Just knock it off and you do know what I mean."

"Yes, sir."

"Goodbye, Greg."

Knock it off was Ruben's favorite expression. It worked for nearly everything. It worked for the occasional on-air happy chatter. It worked for the occasional extremist guest speaking for the Left or the Right, prompting Ruben's signal to slice the interview.

For Ruben there was never any need for an extended conversation, about anything. On politics, skip the bullshit. On race relations, skip the baloney.

Those were his instructions to his staff. He knew it as a writer. Cut everything in half, and then by another half.

On the Middle East, Israel especially, knock it off. Give the Jews a break. They've taken enough. He'd covered the place. He knew the story.

"Thou shalt not pile on," he warned his anchors and correspondents.

* * * * *

There was a knock at the door. A middle-aged fat man came in bristling with obnoxious authority.

Ruben did not like the smile on his face. Neither did Marjorie.

"You do realize that this is Bible country," said the man seating himself comfortably on the unmade bed.

"And?" said Marjorie.

"I'm speaking to the gentleman."

"That's rude," she huffed.

"What the hell is this about?" asked Ruben.

"Let's be clear here…"

"Quickly," said Ruben.

"All right. What was it for, that hundred dollars for my son? I run this place."

Yes, thought Ruben, that had been a mistake, acting on impulse.

"He's a big tipper, my husband."

That too was a mistake.

"Your husband. Do you have proof? IDs?"

"Look," said Ruben. "We paid our money. The rest is none of your fucking business."

"Everything that goes on around here is my business, and, I think I know who I'm talking to," he added, eyeing Marjorie Carmen.

"Your point?" she asked.

"The price has gone up. That's the point."

"Here in Bible country," said Ruben.

"It means we're not as dumb as we look."

Of all the…and we walk into this joint…so thought Ruben.

"Out with it," he said.

"One thousand dollars."

Nobody gasped. They both saw it coming.

"If not?" asked Marjorie.

"I spill the beans."

Chapter 4

Rick got a call back from the local police informing him that he was next in line for a tow truck and an ambulance – half an hour at the most.

Obviously, he thought, there were people in worse shape who needed to be saved first. The rain kept pounding the car.

The pain kept coming and going.

He was confident that Marjorie was doing all she could to speed things up, as was Ruben.

Yes, Ruben. Oh yes, Ruben. The Brit who came to America to show us how it's done. That Ruben.

There'd never been much of a question about those two. How long had it been going on? That was the only question – and were there others? Had there been others? How long had he been playing the fool, the cuckold, the sap? Or...or...or...maybe he was wrong.

I could be wrong, he thought. What's more despicable than a jealous husband? For no good reason. There you go. For no good reason.

Did she ever refuse him in bed? Never. She was a great lay. He was surprised, though, when one night he found that she had shaved between her legs.

"Better for you to lick it," he now remembered her saying.

All that was going into his novel, profanities and all, though the language made him squirm. The thought of her made him glad. But the smut made him blanch. This was not his kind of talk, his kind of writing. He wrote dignified. His first two books contained no such vulgarities and died on the shelves dignified.

Smut sells and you've got to give the people what they want. So, since he knew nothing about cooking or dieting, he'd give them sex.

It wasn't his fault. Sex was there long before he came on the scene. He did not invent the thing. It wasn't like people were having babies from shaking hands and suddenly there he was with something new, like, hey guys, look what I found; you can have babies doing this too, and it can be fun.

People were expecting his next book, this work of his in progress, to be about the broadcast business, focused on his wife. But that would be too obvious and he would never sell her out, not Marjorie, the woman he loved. That would be clear betrayal and a mockery of his very own family.

Joseph Heller had done something like that and it had ended badly for him.

No, Rick Callow was writing something else. It was about Hollywood and how the screenwriter falls in love with the star of his picture.

Naturally, after promising to be his forever, she betrays him. Meanwhile there is plenty of sex.

Obviously for his novel's female character he chose a composite from all the women he had known, and he had known plenty.

But for some reason, they all resembled Marjorie Carmen. It all came back to her. There was no getting around this.

He was hopelessly in love with her in his life and in his fiction. Or was it true what the great John W. Cassell once alleged, that no novelist ever writes fiction. Wow! That was something to think about and not so easy to dismiss. No, there was merit and wisdom in Cassell's proposition.

So onward. Yes, onward for 50 more pages, and here, stuck in the mud, he had pain but he also had a laptop, and he typed and he persisted.

The writing had never gone so well. There was no choice but to write. Thinking of Marjorie hurt and thinking of her helped.

"Use me," she would say. So that's what he was doing, but leaving out many parts that would show her (in the fiction) at her best and only occasionally...well, the other part. Her headlong drive to succeed would pretty much amount to a cliché for an American woman of the 21st century.

Against other women competing with her she was known for her sharp elbows. It was different with men and she knew how to make an entrance, and how to pour it on thick or thin. Of course she was different with men and even with women who could keep her moving upwards.

She was different with him when she thought he was going places. His good looks ("My big bad hunk") were a plus and seen, for her part, as a good career move. They were bound to be Manhattan's newest hot couple and he too knew how to make an entrance and together they were double trouble.

They still made Page Six. They still got seated first, but on her name, not his, and at first he thought, my day will come. The lawyering depressed him and he saw the writing on the wall when he was passed over for partner. He needed something to make a name and thought of acting, the stage, or Hollywood. He'd done some of it in college and before he turned to writing he gave acting one last try off-Broadway in Greenwich Village but never got the callback.

In Hollywood he got cast in two pictures. He was as good as anybody, but not as lucky, so that was that!So, the writing. Yes, the writing. There would be only the writing to make him anything more than her Big Bad Hunk. Marjorie called him a natural and both his agent and his publisher said he had "untapped" talent. But he wasn't fool enough to believe that he had talent or anything else until he produced.

He was no F. Scott Fitzgerald whose words sang across the pages. Nor was he an Earnest Hemingway who built his paragraphs brick by brick.

For Rick it would come through sweat and sheer will. He would get it done, a novel. He began writing it from his heart and writing it true. That was the proper way. There was no fooling the customer. Write exactly how it feels and somehow it will come out all right. People will believe.

He did as he was taught but the people did not believe, not the first time and not the second time. So there goes that theory.

On second thought, the books were good. Everyone agreed. Marjorie agreed and his agent agreed and his publisher agreed and quite a few readers agreed.

He had his loyalists. The online reviews were fine.

What went wrong? Nobody could figure it out and no one dared suggest that he write under his wife's name, which was what they were thinking. He knew it was what they were thinking because he was thinking so himself. Or, now here was a thought that came to him here in the rain – why not a joint byline? They'd share authorship.

What a terrible thought and what a terrible defeat if it came to that, somehow, from someone.

If he'd suggest it to her, well now, that would finish it so far as any respect she ever had for him. That would be groveling and it was doubtful that she would even consent, and if she would consent it would be for pity, which was where he stood with her at the moment anyway.

No, this was his battle and he would have to fight it alone. If he had no talent he would fight to get talent and if he had no luck he would fight to get luck. He would buy it if any of that were for sale and he would steal it if only he knew where to go and snatch it for himself if only for one last try, one last book, that one big book that was destined to verify his manhood.

He kept typing and it kept getting even better. He still got a case of the willies when it was time to insert the erotica. It made him uncomfortable but it had to be done. There was a new readership out there, a new America, new kids who demanded immediate gratification.

They had no patience for subtleties and no time for symbolism, this new generation. They needed everything loud, fast and upfront. He learned from the screenwriters to get the hook in quick and never let go. Pages to Screen were filled with vulgarities and virtually every opening shot began in bed when in times past (and still today) there was nothing sexier than Rita Hayworth removing a glove in "Gilda."

Thinking of Marjorie felt good, always did and nearly always served to turn him on. Those erotic escapades, he'd use them in the book, already had, and let them say whatever they want, he'd meant them for the actress in the novel – could be anybody in real life that springs to the imagination.

Naturally they'd conclude that it was Marjorie who he was exposing, but hell, that wasn't his business.

They'd buzz, they'd snicker, they'd twitter and they'd be wrong and they'd be right.

* * * * *

Damn it felt good to get it all down before it was gone and come on, he was thinking, nothing's gone. What's the complaint?

So quit complaining and stop thinking only about yourself.

He'd get over this too and it wasn't so bad, not terribly bad, and meanwhile she's out there bringing back help.

He had to consider the spot he'd put her in. She too was at risk from this downpour, the worst, the radio kept saying, in over 40 years.

So stop this self-pity and shove the jealousy because, he was thinking, there could be plenty of others besides Ruben Franklin.

He was putting that in, too. He felt good about the novel he was writing. It felt right because he knew his business. From a movie set to a newsroom, behind the scenes it was pretty much the same; the rush of creativity but also the rivalries, the intrigues, the hook-ups that were doomed to evaporate. He knew the score.

He also knew when to stand back and allow a scene to play itself out. He knew his place as it happened between Marjorie and Matt Owens, and Matt Owens, this was the man, the biggest draw at Alpha News and on cable altogether. His ratings were higher than Marjorie's, a fact this blowhard kept reminding his viewers.

He was good. Oh he was good. He was equally good at rubbing it in against Marjorie who'd begun to mount a challenge.

What happened? What was the dispute? He got that in too, but made it between the star and her director. Over what?

Matt had scoffed at Marjorie for being "weak and wimpy" over the interview she'd conducted with a particular candidate for Mayor.

"I'd have handled it differently," Matt Owens had said, and said so across the airwaves.

He had, therefore, ridiculed her as a reporter and as a woman – a woman lacking in cojones.

That one, that one again, still that, even after all the progress, symbolized by Marjorie Carmen herself, but it was still there, the wink.

Marjorie fumed, but kept her rage to herself. Not so Rick. He was ready to go after the son of a bitch, and told her so.

"Don't be silly," she had said. "That would only make it worse."

Absolutely. What? The lady can't handle it herself? Case closed if her man had to step in for her.

Then this – who cared? Reporters did ask her what was going on. Was there really a (delicious) dispute in progress between Alpha's two top anchors?

She'd smile and say nothing or simply, "Everything's fine."

No one asked him. No one asked Rick about the attack on his wife and how he felt about it and if it made him angry enough to do something.

Nobody cared. So he knew his place. Nobody cared what he thought, this drag of a husband.

A touch of humiliation was meant to be welcomed and this time, more than at any other time, he felt heroic. He was suffering in silence, in dignity and in silence and working through the pain. He began seeing it as a test, as fate giving him a chance to prove himself through this accident and through this trial.

Even by losing or come what may he was proving himself honorable and a winner simply through the virtue of putting up a fight.

He wasn't whining. He was writing.

Chapter 5

Later it would be written that the manager of a motel, a man named Leroy Larson, 54, had been the victim of a dispute gone wrong. He was killed. Motive unknown. Police found evidence of a struggle, but no money was missing, so robbery was ruled out. Those who knew him, according to reports, suggested that there had been bad blood between Larson and others around the township. He left behind a wife, Felice, and four sons. But he had enemies, even within his own family. The assailant was being sought, but clues were scarce.

The investigation continues.

* * * * *

"What language is that?" Ruben asked.

"Just what it says," declared Leroy Larson. "Spill the beans means I go to the papers."

"To tell them what?" asked Marjorie as if she didn't know.

"You know what I mean, sweetheart."

"Don't call me sweetheart."

"I'll call you whatever the fuck I want, sweetheart. Or is it babe out there where you come from?"

"My gawd," she said signaling something to Ruben.

Ruben understood the situation. He sure did. But he'd make as if to play.

"After we pay you, what happens?"

"You two get yourselves back to Jew York."

Ah yes, Ruben understood the situation. Jew York. I see.

"Back," persisted the man, speaking to Marjorie, "to you sitting your fanny back in that big chair and showing the world your hot tits."

More: "Love to take a bite out of them tits."

Now here, thought Ruben, calmly, was something quite classic, and he was being entirely calm. Classic in the sense that here was a man so common throughout the world and throughout history. They were like creatures that crawled underfoot and came out of the dark only when provoked by happenstance.

Ruben was especially calm when he came across this type and was known to be masterful under these conditions. He knew this type all right and he knew them when they spoke English and he knew them when they spoke Arabic. Four times, altogether, it ended in blood.

"We'll have to think this over," said Ruben.

Marjorie was startled... but was beginning to understand.

"You mean you want time?"

"Time, yes," said Marjorie, equally calm, as calm as Ruben.

"I'll give you two an hour to talk it over."

"That's right," said Ruben. "Talk it over. This is a big decision for us to make."

"No decision as far as I'm concerned."

"Well it's more than the money."

"Could be," said Leroy Larson heading for the door and out.

* * * * *

Of course no amount of money could keep a man like that from squawking.

"We can't live with a threat like that hanging over our heads."

By that, Ruben meant everything – the ruin of an entire network.

"I don't know what you're thinking," Marjorie said with a trace of concern.

Ruben had arrived from England with something of a reputation, as a man who, elsewhere, may have worked for the Mossad, Israel's secret service. Perhaps or perhaps not, but those were the rumors, and there'd been other rumors about him. Most of those were fantasies, but not all.

He had a Black Belt in Krav Maga. This was fact. He earned it at Pardes Chana directly from Imi Lichtenfeld, the founder of the system. Ruben's first book was on the subject. He taught the system's tactics to both novices and professionals and extreme methods of self-defense he taught only to a few.

Ruben Franklin held certain beliefs that made him dangerous – and now he was dangerous.

He was prone to silence when confronted, before leaping into action. The look in his eyes troubled and thrilled Marjorie.

"Can we get out of this?"

He offered his motto: "Anything is possible."

"You're thinking but I don't know what you're thinking. Do I want to know?" she asked nervously.

He shrugged.

"I know you have a plan. There must be a plan."

He nodded.

There was only the obvious. That man would never be finished.

"It's us or him. I know that's what you're thinking."

She was glad that it was Ruben who was in this fix with her. In no other man would she have such trust. She had chosen well, this particular lover.

"He thinks he has the upper hand," Ruben finally said.

"Well he does."

"For the moment."

"We don't have much time," she said.

"Plenty of time," he said.

She was thinking of Rick as well.

"This is difficult," she said, beginning to sob but stopping it just in time. She must not show weakness.

For Ruben, this was not difficult. This was simple. This was war. That man, that putrid ugly man had declared war upon an entire dynasty.

Alpha News and its 280 affiliates were at risk. One word could bring everyone and everything crashing down.

He was about to insist on her support whatever it was he was going to do, but that would be an insult. Of course she was with him.

But this? Even this?

"I'm going to take a walk," he told her.

"Okay. You mean to think it over, decide what to do."

"Something like that," he said.

Now she was curious, but trusting.

"Okay. You're going for a smoke."

Right. He had his pipe and his pipe helped him think. But he had already done all the thinking that had been necessary.

"You might be in danger for a moment," he warned her and studied her reaction to see if she understood that something was being done.

She was taking it all right.

The man was due back at any moment. "So when he comes in…"

"What?" she said, and still not alarmed.

"I'll want you half naked."

"But you won't be here," she said, now frightened but nearly catching on.

"I'll be around, but out of sight. I'll want him to think you're ready to pay him off with a party."

Now the plan was rounding out.

"It's risky," she said.

"No, it's not. I know what I'm doing. You can do this?"

"I can do this."

"Can you do this?"

"Yes, I can do this."

"That's my girl."

* * * * *

Marjorie felt safe when she had Ruben at her side. She had bodyguards. Russ Appleton made sure of that, but it wasn't Russ and his bodyguards who chopped down a stalker that came lunging at her on Park Avenue. That was Ruben – and it wasn't the first time, no, Ruben kept watch, his fists always ready and there was more than one stalker that had her as his bullseye.

Ruben would be there for her as long as Ruben was around. But he wasn't around when she tested for the job at Alpha News. No, for that she was on her own as were the hundreds who'd swarmed the office for the same job, and one in particular, Sandra Giddings, that anchor woman from Iowa, polished, experienced and professional, already got the job, or nearly so.

Giddings, who came from an ultra-religious home and had prayed for this, had one last hurdle, the Russ Appleton interview. That's what it came down to, Marjorie Carmen versus Sandra Giddings with

Giddings holding the better hand. Everyone knew this. Giddings was in. Marjorie was more beautiful. Marjorie had everything going except experience and for that reason, she was told, it would be best if she'd try another day after some seasoning at some local station.

So it was Giddings who marched out triumphant from Russ Appleton's office and it was Marjorie who knew exactly what she had to do.

She was in there with Russ for more than an hour and though the rumors were plenty there was nothing more to it than Marjorie sitting there with her skirt riding up showing everything without panties. She sold Russ on her personality and on her skills, and on that, too.

Marjorie had made an enemy, but Giddings told it differently, describing it as a mistake, and going on to say, there in the lobby that day, that no career can flourish from such a false beginning. Marjorie was bound to fail, if not now, then later, and that she, Giddings, would always be there haunting her with curses.

Never, she told Marjorie... never underestimate the power of a curse.

Every time you blunder on air, or falter off air, know that I am sticking pins in your heart.

Know that there is no forgiveness for such a grievous sin.

Know that one day when you least expect it a day of reckoning will come calling for you.

You made a mistake.

Marjorie's mistake was listening to the harangue. So she kept assuring herself. She did not believe in curses.

She believed in nothing so fundamentalist and so…so superstitious. Craziness like that belonged to another time, another world.

We were all after the same job and we all did what we had to do. Many had to lose. One had to win.

Marjorie won. She was the big winner. But from that moment on, every time something went wrong, Marjorie wondered.

The curse was always somewhere in the back of her mind.

* * * * *

She was in her bra and panties when Leroy Larson arrived for his payoff, a payoff he had not expected – a gift.

"Anybody home?"

She was in the bathroom, as planned.

"I'll be out in a minute."

He waited, and waited some more.

"What the fuck's going on?"

"You have to give a lady a chance," she cooed.

The man was starting to figure something – his Plan A, really. But even he had thought it to be too farfetched and out of range.

The money, he had figured, was the most they'd give. Things had taken a turn. They settle things differently in Jew York.

Leroy Larson, husband, father of four, a church-goer, every Sunday in his pew, with family, began salivating.

"Where's he?"

"What?" she yelled out still from the bathroom as if fixing herself up for an event.

"Him."

"Who? Oh, he went out for a smoke."

"Signs all over the place against that," he chuckled, his heart beating faster for the delicacy coming his way. "No smoking. Bad habit."

"I know."

Keep him talking, likewise according to plan.

"You coming out?"

"In a minute. You can wait, can't you?"

He'd wait as long as it took. He'd want the money, too. Who'd he tell about this? This would be too much to keep secret.

"Not too much," he said.

"Just a minute," she said.

His breathing turned heavy and his features turned red. But what luck!

* * * * *

She came out in her bra and panties, but made it as if she was frustrated.

He gulped. He had never seen such beauty. On television, yes. In the movies, sure. But real people never looked like that, never.

"Can you give me a hand?" she said. "I can't seem to get my bra hooked up…oops."

The bra fell from her hands exposing her world famous boobs.

He stood there, frozen, unable to move, or unwilling. That was the catch Ruben had worried about.

Suppose he was wise to the scheme.

She lifted the garment off the floor. "Come. Be a man. Help a lady."

He did. He linked the bra back on without touching her.

"Thank you," she said and as he turned to leave, or seemed to move for the door, she thanked him again and said that now she could go back to finish dressing.

She came out fully dressed.

"Sorry for the inconvenience," she said, "and yes, we've agreed to pay you the money. As soon…"

That was the moment he lunged at her and it was the same moment Ruben kicked open the door, grabbed him, slapped him across the face, smacked him senseless in the balls, placed him in a headlock, and twisted his neck, all of it done professionally, by the book, until it snapped. There had been nothing much of a struggle. There was nothing but a dead man who had pushed his luck.

"That was close," she said falling into Ruben's arms, shaken, weeping, still terrified.

Chapter 6

In the worst storm of half a century and getting worse by the minute, airports were closed, planes weren't flying, cars weren't moving and only a few emergency vehicles were getting through. Wherever you were, there you stayed. You stayed put until help arrived.

Power lines were down and even cell phone connections were being cut.

Rick Callow hit on something unexpected. This could be the end. Then it came to him that Marjorie, out on the road or somewhere, could be in the same fix, or worse, all of it his fault. She'd managed to get out but here was the kicker, she'd have been safer, perhaps, if she had stayed in the car.

The mudslide had miraculously pushed the car between two trees that kept it from floating, or from floating down any further. That was the good news. The bad news was that his ankle was still caught in a serpentine maze of interior wiring and terribly swollen and impossible to break free unless he really tried.

He would have to try. Then what? Why then he would manage to get out of the car. Okay, he thought, and then? Why then he'd be able to walk. Wrong. He'd have to wobble on only one good leg. Okay, smart guy, going where? Why, going to stop someone up there on the road.

Aren't you listening? There is nobody up there on the road. There is nothing but rain, wind, slush, mud, thunder and lightning.

"Damn."

Damn where was she? With him, all right, with Ruben, later for that, but for now the life to save was Marjorie's.

How really bad was that ankle? Plenty. Every time he moved it the pain was excruciating. But he had to get out if only to prove that he could.

He'd have to do it in one motion so that all the agony would come at once, as would the risk.

The swelling had stopped, though the coloring of it he did not like, and oddly enough the swelling had the effect of minimizing or dulling the pain.

No chance, he thought, staying like this. Then there was a laptop to save, with his novel in it, and his novel was his life, and the novel was the book on Marjorie Carmen, as it was turning out, unintended. That was how the best novels were written, by the unconscious mind. Like that, Marjorie had taken it over for herself. That had not been the plan.

Neither was this, or that, when he had hit her that one time but only one time. Maybe that was when she took on lovers, if Ruben, or anyone, or just a suspicion or a guess when, one night in particular, he found her lovemaking to be different. Nothing he could explain, but it was different.

So he had slapped her that one time over an argument about desire and temptation and for her part wondering if he ever had eyes for anyone else. No! Back to her, the same question, and she had said, yes, occasionally – occasionally she had fantasies. Anyone in particular?

Okay, she had said, since we're being honest, she named several, plus certain feelings for Russ Appleton and even Matt Owens.

(She did not mention Ruben, as that would be the icing and the fact and the truth.)

"But he's a jerk. I thought you hated Matt Owens."

True, but women are drawn to men in power, she had said.

Well that leaves me out, he had responded.

Well I guess so, she had snapped, and that was when he slapped her.

They made up as they always did.

Then, on a Sunday, when he'd been steady on his laptop, he heard her groaning in the bedroom. She'd been masturbating.

It's normal, she said, without him even asking, and, she added, even within marriage, partners were entitled to private lives.

He'd been hinting about some of that in the book he was writing, and he had her camouflaged through the actress who was standing in for Marjorie on a fictitious movie set that was standing in for a newsroom, where there were trade secrets he'd rather not tell.

There were casting couches there as well and Marjorie had enough to make it on looks and talent alone, but it was more than that when after lunch and then dinner with the boss she landed the morning gig that led to all the rest. She did it on talent, depending on what talent would be most beneficial at the time.

For some it was *you go girl*, but for others it was *simmer down* Miss Hottie Pants.

Of all her adversaries there was one in particular, noon hour anchorwoman Carla Bruin that she, and Rick, suspected of sabotage. Entire scripts were found deleted and often, too often for it to be coincidence, a guest Marjorie had booked for an exclusive – there he was first and exclusively with Carla.

That too was going in, mostly as innuendo, but so much of Marjorie was going in that it troubled Rick at having become so obsessive.

Or maybe he was writing what he was meant to write – the world according to Rick Callow.

Nothing is fiction. The words of the great John W. Cassell.

He was typing when the ambulance came.

Then on the other hand, he was thinking, writing about her so obsessively could be the means to the cure, a way of gaining some freedom.

Not bad. Not a bad thought.

He heard them working their way down, wheels spinning in the mud, traction nearly impossible.

She'd had Henry Kissinger on as a guest. "Power is the great aphrodisiac." That was Kissinger from way back but he repeated it for her show.

So that was what she craved, power in the men she chose and power for herself, and then what? What happens when you have amassed all the power there is to be had? Is there a dead end somewhere? What happens when all your dreams have been met? What's next?

Sounds positively tragic.

That, he was thinking, and writing, could well be the story of Marjorie Carmen. Did she know it, that there really was nothing but a dead end up ahead?

Did she know, for all her on-air cheerfulness, that she was a tragic figure? Deep inside she must know that her life was too good to be true.

She was already losing the glitz of being the biggest deal on Alpha News. But anything else would be a parallel move.

More money? That was a certainty whether she moved on or stayed put. So five or 10 million more per year, what would that prove?

Would prove that she was as desirable as ever. Would prove that her ass had not yet begun to sag.

Because after a certain age it went kaput. The women knew it in Hollywood and it was coming to New York where it was not supposed to be that way, not in the broadcast news business where it was supposed to be – still supposed to be the ageless voice of authority for men or women modeled after Walter Cronkite.

Russ Appleton broke the mold...legs, legs, legs. More than one faded beauty from Russ Appleton's lineup was sent down to cool in the bullpen.

There were rules against that, even laws, but there was also real life and how things really worked.

Even Barbara Walters had it rough among the boys. Marjorie Carmen knew how to roughhouse with the boys and then go wash her mouth with soap.

* * * * *

"Finally," she said.

Finally she had gotten through.

"Where are you?"

"We're coming back to get you."

That was true.

"No need," Rick said.

"Don't need to talk like that," she said.

"I mean they're here," he explained.

"Thank God."

"Where've you been?"

He'd keep it clean and not mention Ruben Franklin.

"Long story," she said.

I'll bet, he thought.

"You'll have to tell me about it someday."

That'll be the day, she thought.

"You don't sound too good," he said.

"Are you in pain?"

"I'm all right."

He was in terrible pain. The words gangrene and amputation kept coming up in his mind.

"Are you angry with me?" she asked.

"Why should I be angry?"

"I don't know," she said.

"Did you do something?"

"I felt awful leaving you in that condition, Rick. I didn't know what else to do. You agreed it was the only chance to bring back help."

Didn't quite work out, he thought, but didn't say. Between them, nothing seemed to work out. This was so typical and so symbolic.

"Aha."

"I think you're angry," she said.

"Can't that wait?"

"So you are," she said.

"I'm fine. Okay?"

"You don't sound fine."

"What do you expect, darling?"

So it was darling.

"I did my best, Rick. I did my best. We all did what we had to do."

"That is so true."

"I wonder what you mean by that," she said.

"Nothing," he replied. "Nothing."

"Can't wait to get you all fixed up and back home."

"Me too, sure. Sure enough."

"I don't like how that sounds."

"There is no other way to put it," he insisted.

"Do you know where they'll be taking you?"

"We'll know when they come. They should be here any second."

"Good. So we'll be heading back to town and be sure to tell me whatever hospital they'll be taking you."

"Of course."

"The minute you find out."

"Right," he said.

"I hope it's not serious, Rick."

"Me, too."

"I'm so sorry, I mean about everything."

He wondered what she meant by that, and certain images formed in his mind, but the first part had been entirely his fault, about the necessity for the trip, to get it straightened out with his ex, knowing that a storm was coming, no need to rush for something that could have waited, and certainly there had been no need to bring her along.

For moral support, he had argued, or was it to prove that she would still do anything for him when he'd begun feeling so extraneous about himself?

Was it to prove that she still belonged to him?

Was it to affirm that, despite everything, he was still her guy?

Was it to confirm that nothing had come between them?

Was it to assure that he was still her big bad hunk?

Was it to verify that she had not given up on him?

Was it to certify that she still had faith in him?

Was it to guarantee that nothing had changed when in fact everything had changed?

"I'm glad to hear your voice," he said, choking up.

* * * * *

Now that was a mistake and the wrong tone against a strong woman, a woman who could not be trifled by emotion on her schedule and what she was up against, a calendar, a clock and a career that was at the mercy of ratings and the goodwill of advertisers and affiliates.

He'd been careful about emotion and about anything that could tip the scales to her advantage.

He knew his role and he knew how quickly and dangerously their roles could shift. He had promised himself to never let that happen.

He was still the man, feminism be damned. Marjorie had no need for feminism. The heavy lifting had already been done for her.

Gloria Steinem and the marches and the sit-ins and the bra burnings had set the stage for her and her generation, a generation that took equality in stride, so that it was even awkward and ridiculous and passé to call yourself a feminist when, look around, so many had it made.

There'd be more hurdles, more complaints, more grievances, more rounds to go, but there was no doubt who won.

Men were doing the dishes and some here and there were proud to call themselves stay-at-home dads, but that would never work for Rick.

Nor for Marjorie.

The attraction had been his virility.

He could never afford to lose that edge.

"Hope you make it back in time," he said, referring to her big catch with the President and the other things she had going.

"It'll be close," she said, "but I'm not worried."

No, on that, on making it click, she was never worried. Somehow everything worked out and even flubs on the air she turned to her advantage.

She knew how to keep it going and how to keep the tech crews rooting for her. They were indispensable and she knew all their birthdays.

"The kids," he began.

"They're fine."

"You checked?"

"Of course I checked."

That one – the one about her being not enough of a mother.

"I was only asking," he apologized.

Not good enough.

"What do you mean did I check?"

"I meant nothing."

"Yes, you did."

"Oh come on, Marjorie."

"Of course I checked. That's the first thing I did."

"Okay, Marjorie."

"Where did that come from, Rick?"

He could have said it came from the pain, or that it came from a series of deeper irritations.

Or that he was only making conversation to keep her on the phone.

That was the main reason.

He had not intended to challenge her role as a mother. She was a good mother. The guilt – that was her own vexation.

So it did not take much to get her riled on the subject.

Between them it was an old wound.

There had been times when she came home too late or too early and they asked for mommy and she'd never forgive herself.

She even told her viewers that her kids come first and they believed her and it was true.

Yes, Rick said to himself, it is true.

The rest is also true, that her career came first. Both came first.

* * * * *

Yes, where did that come from? Now she felt righteous and defensive all at once and she was determined to set him straight.

"I thought we were over that part," she said, as firmly as ever.

"This isn't the time," he shot back.

"That's so old," she went on.

"Agreed, Marjorie. Agreed, and now come on."

This was her sore spot and he had only blurted it out, that was all, but lately he could not seem to get anything right anyway.

He kept making mistakes and each morning when he got up, the first question he asked himself was, what did I do wrong yesterday?

He'd go over the entire day checking where he may have failed, upon whom had he made a fool of himself.

Today who thought less of him because of a slight, an unintended remark, or anything he did or did not do?

What person had he ignored and to what individual or group had he appeared too needy?

Too needy and absolutely groveling and pathetic.

The other person was never at fault. Everything was his fault. Well it sure seemed that way.

He also remembered the book signings where nobody or hardly anybody showed up. Swallow that for a cup of humility. His friends reliably showed up and Marjorie could be trusted to gather up a posse, but the public stayed away in droves even for those book signings in the heart of Manhattan.

He felt properly snubbed and it was the worst kind of reproof when people glanced at him with his books on the table, but kept on walking. Some smiled but kept on walking, and some stopped to flip through some of the pages of his book, but kept on walking, and some, thinking he was the manager or something, asked where they could find the J.K.

Rowling section – or if he could direct them to the bathroom.

He'd never do that again and sometimes he'd wake up in sweat at what it means to be so universally rejected and stamped as a failure and a loser.

No, he'd never put himself through that again and then have to answer to Marjorie, who never wavered in her support. They're idiots. They simply have not caught up to you yet, was what she'd say. He was grateful for her support and ashamed of it as well.

His books did sell here and there, only when the bookstore owner bought them up and presented the bill to Marjorie. He was not supposed to know.

But he knew. It was generous of her and it was generosity she was always prepared to give.

"I thought you were bigger than that," she kept going, now that it was different.

Well, that's how she was when she got started, especially when it was about something so touchy, her responsibilities as a mother. You try balancing two fulltime careers all at once, she kept saying, and let me know how it goes, and in fact he had tried, and kept trying, and it was not going too well.

That was his sore spot and usually she kept clear of it only this time something else was bothering her, the fact that any of this was happening, the rain, the storm, the accident, his ankle, his damn ankle, the motel and what had to be done, and his damn ex-wife who needed to be fixed, herself in the middle of it all for no good reason.

He couldn't have gone alone? Couldn't he do anything alone? None of that was necessary nor would have been necessary had he only, this once, please this once, taken care of his own damn business, as she always did. She had her own ex-spouse and she had her own problems with that bad bargain – he too wanted more – but she never bothered him with her mistakes.

Why, in the first place, had she taken the wheel that drove them into that ditch?

Well, it's true. She wanted to drive. She asked to drive. It was a spanking new Lexus. So that part was on her, and the rest of it, too. She'd done everything she could to get him rescued. This was also true. While the phones were still working she phoned everyone she knew, called in every favor she was owed, and offered any amount of money anybody wanted.

She was not asking Rick for gratitude, but only stating the facts so that later there'd be no misunderstandings or anything like that between them.

There was still this marriage to preserve.

But Rick heard none of that, or only part of that, because they had come, a tow truck and an ambulance together.

He did hear her say, "I love you."

He did hear that, or, he wondered, was it his imagination, because it was what he wanted to hear?

No, she'd said it all right and meant it all right. She did love him. In her own way. Not the same as before, perhaps, but nothing was the same as before.

* * * * *

Later, reports would allege that Marjorie Carmen, the biggest star on all of cable news, had abandoned her husband to the elements, a husband struggling for his own slice of fame. His name was mentioned, a name hardly anyone knew, except that it was her husband, an aspiring novelist.

She was seen leaving, they said, with a Mystery Man.

Chapter 7

She wanted the London network that reached the world. She wanted the world. America had become too local, too parochial, Alpha News too small. She wanted his connections with the network that helped Churchill win the war and that still employed royalty, people named Lord and Sir.

Alpha News had its millions of viewers. The London network had billions.

Ruben Franklin was no fool and wasn't fool enough to think that he'd hooked Marjorie Carmen strictly on his charms.

He'd come over from London and the glamour of it made him sensationally attractive and uniquely desirable.

For Americans there was something about the British. The high-arched accent, that alone was enough to get Americans swooning and believing every word, coming as it did, from the Queen's tongue. Then for Ruben, the wealth, the class, the looks, the success as a broadcaster and the reputation as a writer and as a swashbuckler with a secret past made him quite the catch, though he was married, or maybe not. Another mystery.

There'd been talk about a wife somewhere in France, or perhaps she was merely a mistress. He wouldn't say.

There was much he would not say, but it was fact that he was the son of old money, even titled money, handed down from a dynasty in the lumber trade that began in France in the late 1700s and grew to embrace continents matched only for wealth and power by the Rothschilds.

They began as Jewish but there'd been so much intermarriage, which included kings, sultans, princes and princesses that for Ruben, there was no telling what he was, which suited him fine. He could be Episcopalian, Catholic, Jewish or all of the above, so he practiced no faith in particular, but only one God.

He wasn't strictly British, either. He was born in France. That was where he was expected to stay put and run the family empire.

There was no chance of that and a stopover in Israel changed him. This was followed by an extended stay at a military kibbutz and when the Sabra he fell in love with, Yocheved, and intended to marry – when she was knifed to death during an Arab uprising, this changed him even more.

He remained open to all sides, but there was no doubting whose side he'd taken.

* * * * *

"The smirk," he said, speaking to Greg Olman, his midday anchor.

Ruben got right to it as soon as he got back to New York. He'd forget what had happened only days before in what he sometimes called "the Wilderness," meaning a world that was still so primitive, far less so the United States, but still, they were out there, everywhere.

He would forget if they would let him forget and sometimes his own staff reminded him.

"I don't know what you mean," Greg replied.

Well, thought Ruben, we could go back and forth, and if we do, he wins. They always win. Not always. But often enough. Too often.

Greg Olman had come over from small town local news.

"That sort of business doesn't go around here, Greg."

"Enlighten me."

The son of a bitch and his silver tongue.

"The smirk…"

"Got that…"

"The added opinion, the digs. You're being paid to deliver the news, not to comment."

"I get the point," said Greg, clearly not.

"You do."

"I do. You got people doing commentary and you don't need me."

There he goes, thought Ruben.

"Of course we need you, Greg."

"Thanks," said Greg with the sarcasm.

"This network," Ruben began but stopped. The speech. Everyone knew the speech. Russ Appleton made it nearly every day.

To maintain the public's trust and maintain our credibility, respectability and above all our legitimacy, we must draw a straight line between news and opinion.

That was the speech, but it was more than that; it's what kept the network towering high above the competition.

Russ had fought hard to make it respectable and it was Ruben's job to keep it that way.

That was one reason why Ruben kept hiring them away from big-time print journalism – real journalists, Pulitzer journalists.

These had to be taught the tricks of the trade, to keep things moving short and fast, to get to the point and move on, and to learn how to banter, and how to make friends with the camera, and how to smile through a headache and stay upbeat when you'd rather get back to bed. Always upbeat!

But this was still television and jobs had to be filled and so they came with a dream, reporters and anchors who'd majored not in journalism but in broadcast communications, got their start at some neighborly local station, big town or hick town, and brought with them every cliché imaginable.

Greg Olman was one of those. But he knew his stuff and he had a big voice, a voice that boomed loud enough to make dogs run and hide.

Some complained. They had to turn down the volume.

He was good. He had experience, including the experience of small town prejudices, which he was subtle enough to cover up, but not entirely.

"I don't know what you're asking me to do," said Greg Olman.

"What not to do."

"No, commentary, right. Okay. Fine."

"We've got people to do that," said Ruben.

"Yes, I know."

Greg named Matt Owens, whom he liked. But Greg also named Marjorie Carmen.

"Got no problem with that," Greg continued, though yes he had. "No problem at all, Ruben."

Something about the way he said "Ruben" that irked Ruben. Something small town, backwoods. Something so primitive.

The smirk, the same smirk that crossed his face when he mentioned Marjorie Carmen; the knowing smile that said I know about you two.

Maybe, thought Ruben, he couldn't help himself. Yes, he could. He knew what he was doing, and Ruben knew what the man was thinking.

Ruben had written entire books, bestsellers, about what these people were thinking. Movies had been made from those books. Awards had been given.

If there was to be a snitch in the newsroom it would be Greg Olman, or Carla Bruin who had it in something special for Marjorie Carmen.

"If we're done I should get back to work."

Ruben walked him to the door but extended no handshake.

* * * * *

There was always something else about Greg Olman, always another reason for Ruben to dislike the man.

When news broke about the death of Ed Snider, Ruben sent out a memo alerting everyone to use it on top hour-by-hour to pay tribute to a visionary, a great man. Snider, back in the 1960s, had introduced professional hockey to Philadelphia, a town that still did not know that hockey was played on ice.

Snider had changed all that through the kind of entrepreneurial spirit that Ruben found so uniquely American. To the town, to the nation and personally to Ruben Franklin, who admired big thinking, Ed Snider was a heroic figure. Snider deserved the tribute as did his daughter Lindy and the entire Snider family for maintaining that special touch of class and dignity throughout decades in the public eye.

Lindy, a socialite who never played it snobbish, and was gorgeous to boot, had staged a series of memorials to honor her late father.

But Greg ran all of it as an occasional news clip, and this...this Ruben would never forget.

Chapter 8

The results were mixed when she was moved to prime time. She'd become more controversial by the day so the backlash was to be expected. She'd never make everybody happy and in this business there was no way to please both sides, the left and the right, and she had stopped trying.

That had been a different Marjorie Carmen there at the start. She had won the job but her next job was to win the approval of an audience that did not know her, and she did this by being as measured and as careful as a Miss America contestant avowing "world peace."

She would have to tone down her sex appeal, or, maybe bring it up a notch. She'd figure it out. She always did.

She was behaving like a proper well brought up young lady whom America would be happy to have as a daughter.

Those days were gone. She no longer kept her opinions to herself and mixed it up with everybody.

Including the President of the United States.

The interview had not gone well, or as well as expected, and... "and you do not keep interrupting the President," a heated Russ Appleton told her.

She was in his office, along with Ruben, who thought she had done okay, given the circumstances.

This President, according to Marjorie, liked to make speeches. Somebody, she felt, needed to make him stop long enough to ask the next question.

But two million tweets agreed with Russ.

"What was she supposed to do, sit back and enjoy it, Russ?"

"I resent the insinuation, Ruben. Marjorie, please say something. Anything. Nothing on your mind?"

Plenty on her mind.

"Nothing to say?"

Plenty to say.

Marjorie knew the stakes. The President, this President in particular, might never come back, keeping in mind the grudge he nursed for Alpha News, which he used to ridicule as a joke, as entertainment, a fly-by-night operation until the ratings could not be ignored to keep his own numbers up.

Then there was Russ Appleton. Big as she was, big as she'd become, he was still the boss.

Despite the hoopla, she was an *employee*, salaried into the millions, but still an employee, still on trial as they all were in this business.

One wrong move and her career could turn to dust. Was this the one? No, not likely. There was no one around nearly as good to replace her, and it would take more than one below average interview to get Russ looking around. She was still his girl. But she was on notice.

She was on notice each time she faced the cameras. Every night was another night to perform for a screen test. You never had it made.

Every night was starting all over again.

America watched and waited for any chance to cheer or jeer and plenty of them out there were cheering for her to flop and fall flat on her face.

There'd be no pity for the woman who had it all. She rated some comeuppance. She had incoming from both sides and either side.

There was no neutral side and there was no place to duck and if she'd give in, give her honey instead of her sting, she'd lose the best part of herself and the best part of her audience, people who'd come to admire her for her balls. That was Russ Appleton who told her and the staff to at all times, "Be yourself."

Exactly what she was doing.

"I did what I could," she said, "against the most powerful man in the world."

"If only you'd have quit hassling the man who's trying to fix this country," Russ said, injecting a personal preference.

Only one time had Ruben seen her cry at one of these sessions that Ruben detested – the elaborate and testy post-game hand wringing and blame mongering. For Russ it was necessary. He needed to tear everything down to build it back up again for the next time.

She wasn't crying but Ruben could tell that she was holding it back and saving it for later.

"He came prepared for her, Russ. He came prepared to slaughter her."

"Well he did."

"That's not fair," she said and stormed out of the office.

* * * * *

"I hope you know what you're doing."

"She can take it, Ruben. She's a big girl."

"Not as big as you think."

"She's got to learn the limits. We're only the messengers."

"You went too far, Russ. You hit too hard."

"I'll apologize, but don't you think she's gotten a bit too self-important?"

"Could be."

"Happens to the best of them," said Russ.

"I've seen it happen."

He'd seen it happen even in London.

* * * * *

Ruben had seen something else happen, but it was never to be spoken, that after the fiasco with the President she had broken down.

You'd never know it because she kept showing up on the screen sunny side up.

But people who hated her for no reason now had a reason. The hits kept coming and the hackles arrived non-stop through social media and the regular press, and it was her nemesis from way back, Sandra Giddings, who got it started in a blog alleging "The Other Side of Marjorie Carmen."

In it she kept referring to Marjorie as a tramp who won the job and kept the job only by means of serving up sexual favors.

Giddings provided no evidence, no proof, but the innuendos were enough to kick up a whirlwind of scorn, mockery and derision.

They were out to ruin her, and they nearly did. Her self-esteem was in tatters.

Everybody (it seemed) took a turn analyzing and scrutinizing her bad day with the President of the United States.

She became a target and everybody took a shot.

When the *Post* ran it front page calling her "a lightweight" and "an entertainer" and "not a serious journalist," and then added that Marjorie Carmen was "the shame" of Alpha News together with the rest of cable broadcasting – that's when the migraine headaches came back, along with a case of the hives.

The hate mail and even the death threats, now arriving by the hour, were never enough to terrify her or shake her confidence.

Now it was different and now it was a crisis and Ruben had to rush her to her private and secret doctor.

She always wondered how it would end, serene in old age, or abruptly through illness or a scandal – or anything! She wasn't sure if she was woman enough to take this bullshit or if she even wanted to take this bullshit. She wanted none of it, neither their blessings nor their curses.

She was sick of it, the entire business. What a ridiculous business to be in. We did not deliver the news. We *performed* the news.

Any actor, she was thinking, can take my place. So let them find an actor.

Along the way to the doctor they had to keep stopping to let her vomit. She'd had all that throughout her life, the nausea the worst of it, but had it under control over the past five years, enough to keep her going even when she felt an attack coming on, and just moments before air time. But she was a trouper.

Not so this time.

"Don't talk like that," Ruben had gently scolded her.

She had talked about quitting. She had talked about having no friends, only enemies.

"Don't be ridiculous," Ruben said. "You have millions of friends."

"That's an audience, Ruben. Those are not friends."

"Yes, they are," insisted Ruben, even though he knew she was right.

"Then look what happens after one bad segment, how quickly they turn."

"Only the few."

"Only the few that count, Ruben."

"Don't I count?" he continued, trying to keep her in one piece until she got fixed by the doctor.

"But you love me."

"Yes, I do."

She talked about an entire world being so fickle and how the final tally would show you having one friend at the end of it all – if you were lucky.

The adoration of millions was a joke, she kept saying, an illusion – nothing tangible, nothing lasting, nothing real.

Baloney, she kept muttering. It's all baloney. It's all fake. I'm fake and those friends are fake.

He reminded her again that the hecklers were coming from the other side. She would always have enemies, but mostly loyalists.

"If I quit tomorrow," she said, "do you think it would make a difference?"

"Of course it would."

"None of us are indispensable, Ruben. Not in this business."

"Not in any business...and stop talking nonsense about quitting."

He knew it was nonsense, but he also knew that she was suffering as he had never seen her suffer before. All that, he kept thinking, over a single hour on the air that went wrong, and yes, in this state of mind she was right to imagine that an entire world had gone sour on her.

This was serious. This could be a temporary setback as happened to nearly everyone in the public eye who'd been blindsided and suffered a crash, or, this could be a breakdown of consequence. His attempts to humor her and to console her were not getting across.

She was saying that maybe she could use a vacation. Take a week, a month. But then they'd know they'd gotten to her.

No, that would be weakness. Mustn't let them see you sweat.

Then on the road Ruben had to stop because she was hyperventilating. She could not breathe and had to get out.

Moments later he had to stop the car to put an arm around her to keep her from shivering uncontrollably.

"You look like shit," said her doctor, Dr. Len Crown who saw her at his office on Long Island.

"I can't go on like this," she said.

"You'll live," he said.

"I mean I can't go on the air like this."

He gave her shots for both, but at no more than a quick glance he diagnosed her as a case of severe emotional distress.

He recommended tests.

"No," she said.

He recommended rest.

"Just give me the pills."

That night she was on the air more sparkling than ever. The camera hid everything.

* * * * *

"We have to talk," she said.

"We are," he said.

They were having coffee at the Starbucks down on the corner.

"I don't mean now. I have to rush for the kids. Thanks for standing up for me."

"He was brutal."

"He was just being Russ," she said.

"That's enough. What's the latest? Do you know?"

She knew.

"He was taken to some clinic. It was touch and go but they saved the leg."

"That bad."

"That close, yes."

"So now?"

"Good question."

"Huh?"

"He won't tell me."

"Tell you what?"

"He won't tell me where he is, Ruben. He won't say."

"Am I missing something?"

"That's the story."

"You mean he's in hiding."

"Or maybe," she said, "he's found some peace to get to his novel, away from me and away from everything."

"That doesn't sound so bad."

"If that's what it is," she said.

"What else could it be?"

"You worried?"

"I don't know, Ruben. I don't know. He is my husband."

"If it's the novel, more power to him."

"If it isn't?"

"Your guess, Marjorie, is as good as mine."

"I just hope he's not planning something stupid."

"You know him better than I do."

"I'm not sure I know him, Ruben. I'm not so sure. I'm not so sure about anything when it comes to Rick."

"He's hit a rough patch. All writers do," Ruben suggested.

She let that sink in.

"But is he?"

"Is he what? Is he what, Marjorie?"

"Oh come on, you know."

"I'd rather not say."

"Then I'll say. Is he really a writer?"

"Aha. Now we're getting somewhere."

"You read him."

"His second book," remembered Ruben.

"And?"

"He's okay."

"Okay. I see."

"No," insisted Ruben. "He's really okay."

"I'm not sure what that means."

"He's as good…"

"Or bad…"

"No, Marjorie. He's as good as anything out there on the market."

"You mean it isn't trash."

"Hell no."

"But can he write?"

Ruben had to think about this, about this truly uncomfortable question.

"Okay, since you want it straight."

"Always."

"He can write but he is not a writer."

That was Ruben Franklin at his finest.

"Believe it or not I know what you're saying."

"It's the best I can do," said Ruben.

"What about us?"

"Now that I don't know."

"Or don't care?"

"Please, Marjorie. Before anything you've got to get good with Rick, who's flown the coop, apparently."

"He'll be back."

"What are you telling people?"

"That he's out somewhere recuperating. Nobody really asks. Isn't that a pity?"

"A part of you still loves him."

"A part of me, yes. But what about us? You and me?"

"So is that what this is about?"

"Yes and no. I've got to run. Later."

Chapter 9

He'd been taken to one of those emergency clinics that have been popping up all over those strip malls, since the nearest hospital was too far, and anyway, the guys driving the ambulance were plastered and only wanted to get rid of him. They demanded cash on the spot and since he had no cash but only the credit card, they drove him first to an ATM machine to get the cash.

They did carry him into the clinic and dumped him down on a bed and left counting their money, since that part cost more.

There was no doctor in the house, only a nurse practitioner and her assistant. The nurse practitioner was named Iris. She was not beautiful but not unattractive, either. There was, at least through Rick's eyes, something quite erotic about her rounded figure and caring approach. A caring touch, that felt like something new, something he'd been missing. Where's that been?

"You'll need to see a doctor," she said after examining him, "but we'll see what we can do in the meantime."

"Anything will do, just please stop the pain."

She gave him a shot of something and told him to relax. Then she said that before working on the ankle and mending it as much as possible, he'd have to wash up from head to toe to cleanse off the grime all over his body. She asked if he could make it to the shower and then, on second thought, decided that no, he couldn't.

"You'll have to trust me," Iris said. "Don't worry. I've seen it all."

She took off everything except his shorts, which showed an erection.

"It's natural," she said, businesslike.

She scrubbed him clean and as she did so, she asked him how did this happen, who he was and where he was from.

"You'll have to fill that out?"

"Unless you won't want me to," she said.

"I'd rather you didn't."

"I understand," she said.

Then the ankle. It was not broken after all, but badly sprained, according to her diagnosis.

The swelling was the concern. She gave him a shot of penicillin and patched him up. He sure liked her touch.

"I'd say you were a day away from gangrene," she declared.

Just as he had it figured.

She took his temperature and it was awfully high. If it failed to go down within an hour or so there'd be no choice except to get him to the hospital, which was overcrowded because of the storm and there was no telling what was going on at the emergency room.

He did not dare ask why, therefore, this clinic was not more crowded. She read his mind.

"The truth is," she laughed, "we don't have a good reputation."

"Oh."

"Comforting, isn't it." She smiled and kept patching him up.

"I think you're joking."

"Actually, we've already taken care of hundreds and sent them home or to the hospital. You're our last victim. We close up in ten minutes."

* * * * *

He'd begun nodding off and when he awoke found himself in someone's home, a farmhouse in farm country.

"We didn't know what to do with you," she said when he awoke.

She explained that she had no choice except to go through his wallet where she found the usual, even next of kin, but knowing...well knowing what she knew about life, she chose to take no chances just in case something else was going on, and since back at the clinic he declined to be identified, she sensed that he must be in some kind of trouble.

His next of kin was his brother. There was no information in his wallet to suggest that he was married to the sensational Marjorie Carmen.

He was his own man.

There were pictures of him together with Marjorie, but that could mean anything since other women were in the same photos.

"Are you? In some kind of trouble?" She regretted the breach of etiquette the instant she blurted it out.

"Not what you think," he assured her, and here in her home surroundings he found her to be sensationally attractive.

She was wearing ordinary shorts and a sweater, but there was nothing ordinary about her figure. He especially liked the slant of her boobs. Again that problem came up, the problem that had embarrassed him back there at the clinic, but here, he guessed, there'd be no need for those supplements that he'd required, lately, but only lately, to get it going with Marjorie.

"You're married," Iris said.

"Yes."

"Shouldn't..."

"No need," Rick said.

"I get the picture," she said.

She took his temperature and thank God it had gone down along with the swelling.

"You'll live," she said.

* * * * *

He didn't ask. She didn't tell. He wasn't even curious to know who she was, who she really was, or what she did, what she really did.

"They saved your laptop," she said.

"I know."

"Are you a writer or something? Never mind. I shouldn't have asked."

She had given him sleeping pills and he was drowsy but not enough to fall asleep.

"You can't seem to relax."

"I don't know what it is."

"I know you're from New York and those people are always tense."

That, he thought, and so much besides.

"We need to get you back in shape," she said. "You're now my responsibility. You know what they say."

"No, I don't."

"If you save a life you owe your life to them forever. You are quite handsome. I like you."

How refreshing, he thought. No artifice. No tricks. No games. No beating around the bush. Nothing sophisticated.

"I like that one," he said.

"Which one?" She laughed.

"All of it," he said.

"Now," she said sternly, "how are we going to get you to relax?"

"Another sleeping pill?

"That doesn't seem to do the trick. Not with you. Here, let's try this."

He was ready. He was as ready as a stallion when she pulled down his shorts and got busy.

* * * * *

There'd be no messages coming in or going out. He'd make himself a recluse, an author in retreat. He stopped shaving, grew himself a beard. She liked that look. She liked everything about him. She liked to hear him talk when he felt like talking. She liked his smile. She liked his touch. His touch did something to her.

She suspected that there was something important about him and that he knew important people, but she was determined to know no more about him than what she already knew, that he was a writer, but there'd be no Googling for her, which would spoil everything.

He was her secret, her dirty little secret, and it never failed with him. When she got home at night there was no stopping them. Once in a while, caught in reverie, she'd rush home during lunch when she felt the need and he knew her specialty and was always ready.

He kept typing. The pages he'd never had a chance to save he'd have to do over again, but it was never the same as the first time.

But maybe better, or maybe worse. But he kept on typing. She liked that too, how serious he was when he got to work. He'd forget to eat. He'd forget the hour, the day, the week or the month. He seemed to want it that way, and he was best that way, whether he was working or just lounging.

Money was no problem. That was fact. He told her that if she wanted to quit her job, he'd support her.

He did not tell her that he had four and a half million dollars banked in his name, but through his wife, but never mind.

Much of it was in stocks, which he could cash in at any time, and he would not care about penalty charges.

To hell with all that. To hell with everything.

* * * * *

Iris was a reader, it turned out – a lover of books. She was an associate something or other at the library, a volunteer. This part of her came out gradually. Her job was to read the newest books that came in from the top authors and publishers and to suggest to Miss Hogan, the director at the library, which of them ought to be showcased.

She enjoyed the work, but she did not care for much that was coming in. Her favorite author was F. Scott Fitzgerald. There was nothing like him around these days. She liked his writing and she liked his suffering, that is, his suffering for his art, through the alcohol and through abiding a mentally ill wife. She'd read all about that, all his autobiographies, and how Zelda, before she was institutionalized, would try to ruin his work from spite and jealousy.

He was out of print and nobody asked for him at the library. There were a few copies of his books on hand but they stayed put in the shelves. Her favorite book of his was not the one that made him famous at such a young age, *This Side of Paradise*, but the one he wrote as a series of essays about being down and out, *The Crack-Up*.

She felt for him, still, as though he were still alive and still suffering, and she'd never forget, line for line, what he wrote as a form of surrender, where after a certain date he would save his virtues for himself, as a man and as a writer, but give nothing of himself to the public. He would offer the necessary smiles, make the appropriate gestures, but it would only be a performance.

He'd given up, but not on himself, but on his friends and the world, or maybe all of it together.

She felt the same way about Rick, though she wasn't sure why, except that defeat was written all over him. She knew, she sensed that at one time he must have been a man going places, a man of promise. Then something happened. She would not ask. One day she'd find out if there was anything to find out and if he'd be willing to give.

She'd rather not know. Not knowing had been working for them, beautifully. Knowing too much about somebody, of that she'd had her fill. Not that again. But this one was different. There was a touch of the aristocrat about him, that touch of class. He carried himself that certain way.

The doctor who had come to treat him, Dr. Hy Mendes, her uncle, had taken her outside to ask what this was all about.

She couldn't explain or she did not want to explain over his concerns about a stranger she had taken in.

This was a stranger she had taken in as a lover and he warned her about the world.

Well she knew about the world and she would trust her instincts.

Mendes warned her about her instincts. Her instincts had betrayed her before.

Not this time, she said. This time she was sure and she knew what she was doing.

* * * * *

Rick did nothing, over the days and weeks, to make her think she'd erred. They never quarreled. He gave her money for food and clothes, but refused to go out with her, shopping or anything else. He refused to go out, period. Some days he just stayed in bed, thinking.

Well he did go out with her now and then for some McDonald's, but would remain in the car, and caution her to drive carefully and to avoid ditches.

One day it happened that he did go out with her to what was still called the Village Square. He needed batteries for his laptop and other supplies. His beard and long hair and shaggy clothes would cause no sensation in this part of the country, but something changed when a woman in the drugstore seemed to recognize him, and it got worse when a man said, "Hi," as if he knew him.

She did not ask him what was wrong when she found him back in the car with a case of the chills.

"Can you imagine that?" Rick said. "The man tried to touch me."

This wasn't true, but Iris would let it go.

"Did you know that woman?"

She wasn't sure which one because beard and all, he was an attractive man.

"Which one?" She laughed.

"The one who was staring at us."

That had been so fleeting that it had made no impression on Iris.

"No, I don't."

"Well she was staring at us."

Iris wondered if there was a woman, a woman somewhere, who was behind all this. If so, bless her, because now she, Iris, had him.

Most likely it was a woman as Iris had it figured. Her intuition told her so, that this woman, somewhere, had done serious damage.

That was pure speculation, but good enough for Iris. There was no telling what had happened, a particular blow or a series of events.

Well she would nurse him back until he came to himself, but she did not want that, either. She wanted him as he was.

She did not want him to find what he had lost and to recover his past. That would return him to everything he had been and ruin everything.

* * * * *

"Is there anything I'm not doing?" he'd begun to ask her.

"Like what?"

He paused, thinking deeply.

"In some way am I disappointing you?"

The tone of it worried her.

"Not at all."

He was sitting at the kitchen table working the laptop, the novel, it seemed to her, humming along.

Often enough he did the writing on the couch or in bed, but when he moved to the table it was serious, serious writing.

He became absentminded when he wrote or when he thought about the writing. She found it charming. Her absentminded professor.

He said, "So you find me adequate."

Where did that come from? Was it something she had said, something she had done? Was this to become an argument, their first?

She looked at him searching for a smile or a frown, but he was expressionless. She wondered if she ought to pursue or let it drop.

But adequate was a dangerous word.

"I don't know what you mean."

He'd had a few drinks, but nothing more than usual, the scotch and soda. Were there sides of him still to come?

She doubted this. She trusted him. She was all in.

"I mean, dear Iris, am I good enough, you know, adequate."

That sounded sharp.

"Rick, what is it?" she asked, finding herself feeling cornered. The happy house had turned gloomy.

He went back to typing as if to forget the whole thing, or as if to give the matter no more importance, but she knew that something was not right.

"If I told you how I really feel," she said, with emotion, "I'm afraid you'd bolt."

He kept on typing. Then he stopped. Took a shower. Then sat down next to her, took her hand and held it tightly.

He kissed her gently. It was that kind of a kiss. Not the other kind that meant business. This one meant warmth.

They did enough business. It was their specialty and it never became routine. In bed she gave up everything. So did he.

He'd bolt if she told him she loved him. That's what she thought but she would be wrong. He'd welcome it, but he did not want to hear it, either.

He'd heard those words before. In the meantime he wanted no dramas.

"Don't mind me," he said. "Must be something I'm writing that's got me going."

He was writing about Marjorie Carmen. That was enough to make anyone feel inadequate.

* * * * *

The novel was beginning to take shape, he'd reached the point of no return, the point where an author knows he's gone so far, so true, that to quit would be like murder, like killing a living thing. So now he had a living thing and was beginning to feel a sense of achievement.

Only he knew what they'd say, that once again he was cashing in on her. He knew that's what they'd say, but it would be wrong. He was writing what was being given to him. He believed that's how it worked. For others, like Hemingway, it was write what you know. Good enough. But for him it was write what's being given to you, and if that sounded too mystical, let them scoff.

They would, too, and this time there would be none of her friends to rush to his defense. Quite the contrary.

They'd go after his hide. They'd accuse him of being a gold-digger and a bloodsucker and even if he used a pseudonym, they'd still figure it out.

Or maybe not. He might come up with something to keep him out of the picture.

He sometimes thought that it might be enough to simply have it written and forget about getting it published. There was no law saying that everything you write must be published, so maybe, he sometimes thought, getting it down would be enough. Glory? Was that what he sought?

Probably. Yes. He had to admit that glory would be nice, very nice.

Was it revenge he was after?

That is where it got touchy with him. That's what they'd say. They'd say that all right. They would be wrong.

Would they?

He had to be honest with himself about this and surely at times that's what he had in mind, but ruin was never his plan.

That would not be a plan for someone you loved and he still loved her, loved her sweetly, delicately and passionately.

The beard did not disguise that fact.

Iris did not change that fact. He felt deeply and erotically about Iris, but it was different.

Iris was home. But Marjorie was fantasy. Iris was heaven. But Marjorie was the hell every man sought.

Fine. He'd live with the fantasy, that once upon a time...but he would never relent or reconcile. He'd be firm about this.

He'd refuse her even if she went down on her knees begging, which she would not do, of course, but he could dream, couldn't he, and the dream would be enough, and even the book would be enough, published or unpublished, because he was done with that life.

Then, whoever said that a novel had to be finished? Nothing made him happier than the writing, the creative process as they had it in the lecture rooms.

But suppose, he sometimes thought, the writing was done. Then what? What would there be left to do? Another book?

Doubtful.

No, this was the book, the only book he had left.

So that was a serious consideration, to keep writing for the sake of writing and for the sake of writing Marjorie Carmen out of his system.

He would make her wholly fictitious and pine for her as men salivate for unapproachable princesses of the screen.

She would stop being real and he would only glance at the memory of her and the memories they shared and if it hurt, let it hurt.

He was resolved to be a new man, distant from everything, himself unapproachable.

* * * * *

Iris was glad to notice a change in him. He became more talkative and allowed her to put on the TV. The TV was always on, but only for the movies, never for the news. Never the news, local, regional, national, international and besides the fact that nothing even changed anywhere around the world, he had his reasons, other reasons.

He gave in, that one time, to watch C-Span, the section on books, and it went downhill when a reviewer showed up who had panned his second book, so that was the end of C-Span for Rick or anything to do with books or politics and he was up all night thinking of that man, that reviewer and so many other reviewers.

But she knew the writing was going well and that he was totally lost in it and happy. The tension that had toughened his face on the brow and around the edges had dissolved. The distracted faraway look in his eyes made him as beautiful as he was handsome. He radiated.

He was getting out more around the house, walking with a cane. He walked around the woods and became known around the neighborhood – no more as a stranger, or *that* stranger among adults who worried about their children. He was well liked. People smiled and he smiled back. It was accepted that he was different, a man who talked to himself, a man deep in thought.

There'd been some people with New York license plates snooping around, asking about him, but they wouldn't tell, thanks to Iris.

She had told the neighbors that bill collectors were pursuing him and to expect such intruders and to please keep them out and off the grass.

They were happy to cooperate. Bill collectors, tax collectors, moonshine heat, this was something they all understood.

Iris noticed something else. He did have a temper and he let it loose when there was a knock at the door. This terrified him.

It interrupted his work, he explained, but there was something else about it that he could not explain.

* * * * *

The man in cowboy hat and cowboy boots, arriving on a motorcycle, came in with a key. Iris was late because it was her usual night at the library, and this day they were running a contest for members and staff to select the three greatest short stories from American writers. This was no contest for Iris.

She chose Irwin Shaw's "The Girls in their Summer Dresses." Shirley Jackson's "The Lottery." Ernest Hemingway's "The Short Happy Life of Francis Macomber."

Chapter 10

Clash of egos, thought Ruben, sometimes that was the only part of the job, keeping them apart, these prima donnas.

What a bunch of babies! This wasn't Hollywood and the studio system. This was New York and the newsroom system and it is not supposed to be about stardom around here, only the news, that's why we're here, to be the messengers and nothing more, like the BBC did it when the BBC was good.

He'd left London just in time, but never expected the diva culture that he found once he got to the United States and Alpha News.

Cry babies.

Every day another closed-door complaint from someone feeling unappreciated or underappreciated or this new one, upstaged.

Them and their fat contracts, they did not know how lucky they were. They could all be replaced. Well, not all of them. No, not all of them.

Marjorie Carmen's contract was due for renewal and Marjorie Carmen could not be replaced.

Some, like Carla Bruin, had tried, and failed. Her

nights subbing for Marjorie sunk the ratings.

Carla tried, even tried some of Marjorie's mannerisms, but only Marjorie could do Marjorie. She was still Chick Power Queen. (She preferred "princess.")

This was rare. She was a rare one.

So now what? Was it really her fault?

* * * * *

"He won't call on Bill," Russ Appleton was complaining, "and that's bad for us. Very bad. Awful. Fucking awful. A nightmare."

A nightmare for Russ was a nightmare for Ruben.

Bill Warlington was the network's man in Washington, its White House correspondent, super at his job but the President failed to call on him during his latest news conference and the snubbing was no secret; word had been making the rounds for days that the President was preparing to stiff Alpha News from now till doomsday after the Marjorie Carmen debacle.

Or disaster, as Russ Appleton chose to call the rebuff that could become a White House boycott against the entire network.

The affiliates were already howling. Bill Warlington had paid his dues to get himself accepted – and now this!

Over an interview that had been botched.

Things like that, a White House cold shoulder, never happened to the other networks, the "real ones."

That's what Bill was thinking, but he would never put it like that to Russ Appleton. He didn't have to. Russ was thinking so himself.

For Russ, from day one, it had been about legitimacy, first, and prestige, also first. He finally won on both counts but it was a triumph that kept teetering.

The buzz around town was that the President would never appear with Marjorie Carmen again. Well, he'd said so before as a candidate.

But now he was President.

Neither he nor anyone else from his administration would ever show up for Marjorie. That was the buzz.

That was more than buzz. The President, still a tweet junkie, had it posted as, "Forget her," and everybody knew what he meant.

"I'll get this fixed," Ruben promised Russ.

"How?"

"I'll figure something out."

"Don't forget that this goes way back between these two."

These two meaning Marjorie Carmen and the President of the United States and how awful she'd been to him when he was running for office.

Well he thought so. She didn't. She was doing her job as a journalist. Tough questions come with the territory.

But he thought he was being singled out and picked on. Many thought so.

"She'll find a way to make up to him," Ruben was saying. "She has her ways, you know that, Russ."

"Not with this guy."

"He's relented before," said Ruben. "He'll relent again. He needs us."

"Oh?"

"Even he needs numbers."

"But for us it's life and death, Ruben."

* * * * *

There was a time when Matt Owens would share a table with Marjorie Carmen over at the cafeteria and there was a time when they shared gossip and birthday parties, all that and more, but no more. He used to promote her program, the hour slot after his, and they'd tussle publicly over that and this, but all as part of good clean fun. But no more.

Their friendly rivalry over politics was good for Matt and good for Marjorie and good for the network all around, but when the rivalry turned out to be about ratings everything changed and Matt became spiteful. Matt's ratings had been tops going back 15 years and when Marjorie came along, this fresh face, he was glad to be her biggest booster.

He was glad to give the little lady a big hand.

But when her numbers began climbing and nearing his numbers, that's when Matt stopped being her friend.

The cooling was obvious inside the house and out, but no one thought much of it until Matt took it a step further and began needling her, nothing much, only dropping a hint here and there, telling his audience that whatever she had done the night before, well, he would have done it differently.

The interview with the President, he would have done that much differently. He announced that publicly.

Privately he told Ruben, "Pray that he doesn't brush me off, either."

The President liked Matt Owens, about the only reporter or anchor he did like on Alpha News. He showed up for Matt quite often.

Fortunately, the next visit was still set and no talk of getting it cancelled.

"So no harm," Ruben told Matt when Matt came storming in.

"What was she thinking?" asked Matt rhetorically.

"She's still learning."

"She's had enough time," said Matt.

Matt, nobody liked. Nobody around the building. He was feared, but never respected. People had to act friendly to him because his show brought in the biggest number of viewers by far, except for Marjorie's, who'd been closing in. But he was still number one and he'd let nobody forget that fact.

Even Russ Appleton feared him. Matt Owens gave the company everything Russ Appleton craved, legitimacy and prestige. Russ was kept up nights worrying about what would happen if Matt ever decided to leave, but strangely, very strange, Matt had no offers. None of the other networks had ever extended an invitation for an interview or even for drinks to discuss what he might have in mind for a next step.

Nobody liked Matt Owens except for the 15 million people who tuned into him every night.

That was three million more than Marjorie Carmen's numbers, and she kept creeping ever closer.

"What the hell do you want me to do, Matt? What's done is done. The girl had an off night. You've had those, too."

"No I haven't."

"Matt."

"Name one."

"Listen..."

"Name one off night, Ruben. Go ahead. I'm waiting."

Well fuck you, mister. Maybe once, if his numbers ever slipped, slipped badly enough, Ruben would be able to say that to Matt.

But Matt Owens was still tops. There was no sign of his losing his audience. There was a reason for this. Matt Owens was good. That was the reason.

He knew how to move a show along and how to cut a guest when a guest got to speech-making. He knew how to talk to academics, entertainers, politicians and best of all, the President against whom he'd never be impertinent. Matt was not known for subtleties or for having a soft touch, but for the President, yes.

"Exactly what is it you want?" Ruben asked Matt.

Ruben tried to like Matt. He tried it every day. There really was no good reason to dislike him, no good reason at all.

He was arrogant? So were they all.

He was self-absorbed? So what else is new?

He could be catty, vindictive...we all have those days.

Was he the newsroom snitch? No, that was midday anchor Greg Olman.

So there was nothing in particular to dislike about Matt Owens. Nothing to dislike except that the man had no class.

He had everything else going, but no class, and there was no defining class. You had it or you didn't.

Class, Ruben knew, you could not borrow or buy or steal; it was there or it wasn't. Sometimes it could be obtained with a British accent.

That's why he'd dropped his, as much as he could, but around the building it was accepted that Ruben Franklin had class.

There was nothing like old money to get class, and Ruben had that, too, and he had the gift of being liked – liked, respected and often adored.

He'd been offered an anchor's chair, as he had it in London, but he declined. The real news-making was behind the scenes.

That's where real journalism happened.

The rest was acting.

Their credentials could not be denied, but it was still acting, with all the melodrama that went along with acting.

They needed to be loved.

There was no journalism in that!

None at all, Ruben kept reminding himself.

To be loved was that other business, that frivolous business.

That's why Ruben disdained awards and award ceremonies for journalism. This was not supposed to be about competition.

This was supposed to be about keeping the public informed and to Ruben's thinking there was nothing more important.

A misinformed or uninformed public could be deadly. Could lead to chaos.

So shut up and just deliver the news and if it's opinion you were hired to do, give it and then shut up as well.

"It's nothing that I want," insisted Matt Owens. "But I would suggest that she should be monitored more carefully."

"Monitored?"

"I mean that her guest selection ought to be previewed, so that this doesn't happen again. She's not prepared for the big boys."

"She does enough big boys and she does very well," Ruben shot back.

"Not this time she didn't."

"That was unusual. That was one time."

"I can think of other times."

I'm sure he could, thought Ruben. I'm sure he could.

He probably keeps a ledger.

"Come on, Matt. You know I'd never do that to you or to her. You've both been doing very well with Laurie on assignments."

Laurie Pilgrim was managing editor.

The boss stepped in and sat down.

"I know what's going on here," said Russ Appleton, "and I can't run a business with unhappy campers, Matt."

He'd come to ask Matt to quit the tattling, and that if he can't say anything nice about Marjorie, so please say nothing at all.

People don't have to know that there's a spat. Everything was moving along fine, just fine.

So whatever happened, happened.

Don't need the back and forth – though from Marjorie's point of view it was coming from one direction.

That could change.

"I was telling..."

"I can imagine what you were saying, but this has to stop. People are talking. People have noticed and there's chatter."

Matt laughed. "Nothing wrong with chatter."

"Won't do in the long run," said Ruben. "We don't want people laughing."

"Exactly," Russ agreed. "Doesn't take long until all that buzz between you two turns to mockery."

"Talk to her," said Matt. "Not me."

He got up and stormed out.

"We've got a problem," said Russ.

"I know," said Ruben.

* * * * *

It did change.

Marjorie jumped on Matt Owens for giving the Israeli speaker no chance to talk, no shot to make his case.

"Shouldn't a debate give both sides equal time?" she asked her millions of viewers. "Huh? Come on, Matt. Play fair."

This was the first time she'd gone after Matt Owens.

She wasn't smiling, either.

* * * * *

"What the fuck?"

"Is this a question from my news director or from my lover," she asked Ruben, laughing.

"Both."

"I need coffee."

"Coffee is the last thing you need."

But they ended up in the usual Starbucks.

People came up and congratulated her. Served him right, the pompous jerk.

"I just couldn't take it anymore," she was telling Ruben. "Who does he think he is?"

"Well you know what he is."

"Besides that," she said.

She meant his numbers.

"Besides that there's nothing," said Ruben.

"I hope you're wrong."

"I hope so, too," Ruben agreed.

"We still haven't had that talk," she said, changing

the subject, a subject he knew that was bound to come up.

There'd been hints of it for some time. This appeared to be the time.

"So talk."

She turned sheepish. She blushed those big bright beautiful green eyes.

"There's something I've been meaning to ask you."

"Yes, I know."

"You know?"

"I've known it for some time," he said.

"Like what's been going on?" she asked.

"Yes, and what you plan to do about it," he said.

She let that sink in, not quite ready to plunge ahead. He seemed to be a step ahead of her all the time, this lover of hers.

"So you're thinking for both of us? Is that what I'm hearing?"

"No, I'm thinking what you're thinking."

"Hah," she laughed. "Now you know what I'm thinking."

"Now I do, yes."

"Which is?"

"That you want to pack up and leave for England."

She grew flushed.

"I don't know what to say."

"Did I guess right?"

* * * * *

They moved the discussion back to his apartment. She made him lunch. They showered together. They made love. Then he showered again.

She wondered why. She always wondered why. She wondered why men, all her men, always needed that post-coital shower.

Was it something from ancient times? Were women still "unclean?"

"Well you know how it's been going in the newsroom," she said.

"You mean you and Matt."

"Me and everybody."

"Huh?"

"Something's been going on," she said.

"Nonsense."

"How British," she laughed.

"Nothing's been going on. You're imagining too much."

"I'm not imagining Russ Appleton. He's taken Matt's side."

"It's about nobody's side, Marjorie. It's about protecting the brand."

"Well I have to protect myself."

"Out with it," Ruben said.

"You want it straight?"

"Come on, girl."

"Can you get me to the BBC?"

She expected a bigger reaction. She got no reaction, except a fatherly smile.

"Well now..."

"You don't seem surprised."

"Are you kidding? I've been waiting for this for some time."

"You're too smart for me, Ruben."

"I'll see what I can do."

Her features blossomed back to girlhood.

"You think something can be done?"

He nodded, took her hand and kissed the tips of her fingers. He felt fatherly. He felt like the father she'd never had.

"What I think," he said, "is that you think you've outgrown the network. That's what I think."

This was awkward for her because this would make it appear that this had been her plan from the start, that she had been scheming, the oldest accusation in the book for women like her. In fact the plan had come late, and for many reasons, among them her restless nature.

Then of course the new, and sometimes old, tension in the newsroom, colleagues who've begun taking sides...rumors of affairs...the usual backbiting from fellow anchors like Carla Bruin... the silent treatment from Greg Olman and his claque... and mostly of course Matt Owens.

Or mostly perhaps it was the boss of bosses Russ Appleton whose betrayal, real or perceived, stung her the most.

Her contract was soon expiring. Time to make a move, perhaps. She had other offers. She'd already had lunches and even dinners with execs from all the other networks. She was in play. The money was big.

No matter how big, Russ Appleton was sure to match and exceed the going rate to keep her.

She'd been tempted, and flattered by all the attention, but whatever move she'd make would still be parallel, whether from ABC, NBC or CBS. She'd be getting a bigger slice of the American pie, the traditional networks, despite dwindling shares, still outdrew cable triple-time, but she'd still be starting from scratch and compelled to win over an entirely new audience – middle America that wanted mostly the top story, the weather and nothing much besides, and whose attention span was short for all the political infighting in which she excelled.

* * * * *

So Ruben was right and he was wrong. Yes she had outgrown the network, but it was more complicated than that as it always was with her.

There was no outgrowing America, but to her thinking the time to leave America was before the time America had had its fill of her.

Marjorie always pointed to Oprah as the TV icon who knew when it was time to quit them before they quit you.

"I've never wanted to come straight out to ask you directly," she told Ruben. "But..."

"But it's like you've been using me."

"You know I love you, Ruben."

Those words never came easily to her. So she meant what she said.

"Okay," he chuckled.
"That's funny?" she huffed.
"No. But the timing."
"By the way, do you realize something?"
"What?"
"You've never said you love me."
"Yes, I have."
"No, you haven't," she insisted petulantly.
"But I do."
"Never mind. It would only come out wrong if you tried it now. Timing, you know."
He'd gotten her in a mood.
"Timing," she repeated.
"Marjorie," he pleaded.
"Timing," she said.
"I only meant...hell I've forgotten what I meant."
"Let me remind you. Timing."
"We seem to do that fine in other sports," he teased.

She smiled. He had her back. He did love her. Was it true? That he never told her so? He'd have to get this right. But there never would be getting it right. There could be no future with a woman like Marjorie Carmen. No chance. So he kept his cards down and tucked in.

He'd go with it as long as it lasted, and it was so good while it lasted, better than all the rest.

He'd hate to have it end, but he'd be ready when it happened. So he'd never jump in with both feet over someone like Marjorie Carmen.

He was too smart, too experienced, and on more than one continent. He'd been around. He'd dated princesses.

This too was a princess. But in some ways they were all the same, overbearing and unreliable.

These were the kind that launched a thousand ships, but not the kind that nurtured a nest.

"Be honest," she said, now entirely honeyed.

"Okay. I'll try."

"You never did take me seriously."

"I think you're the best I've ever come across. What are you talking about? Don't you dare start getting insecure on me now."

"I'm not talking business."

"Oh."

"I'm talking you and me."

He usually avoided the topic, with all his women. Well, the truth was, he didn't believe in love. Not the kind people talked about.

Not the kind that made the world go round, if you believed that horseshit. No, it wasn't love that made the world go round.

So she was insecure, and not about business. About love.

"But me and the BBC," teased Ruben.

"I feel terrible for having been so obvious for so long."

"Good. We're talking business."

"Fine. I need to move on."

"You mean do I still have connections."

She had another question in mind as well, quite strange.

"Ruben, this might sound crazy. But do they even know me over there?"

An incredible thought from one of the most famous women in America, but a logical question, entirely appropriate.

Good question, this. Big as she was over here, was she small potatoes over there, and while he'd been there, he'd never heard her name come up. Nor had the Alpha News network ever come up, nor, come to think of it, had any of the other American networks ever come up, save for something late breaking.

The BBC was the biggest in the world, but of a particular world, somehow insular. The United States was seldom topic number one. The focus was on Africa, Asia, and the Middle East. They had not yet discovered America, not quite yet, over there at the snotty BBC.

But Marjorie Carmen wanted it because she figured it to be the world, and Marjorie Carmen wanted the world.

She had every right. She had paid her dues.

"I don't know," he said. "Damn. I really don't know."

"Well isn't that a wake-up call," she said, "for those of us who think we're the hottest thing on the planet. Wow."

Yes, wow.

Chapter 11

"So, I hear you're a writer or something."

"Or something," said Rick to a man who had just invited himself in while Iris was doing overtime at the library.

"I'm Chuck."

She had never mentioned Chuck, but then, she had never mentioned anybody, which was part of the deal from both of them. But of course, thought Rick, she'd had a life before he came along, any kind of a life, perhaps a Chuck kind of a life. Chuck wore chains and tattoos.

"She out somewhere?"

"Obviously."

Chuck didn't take the hint, that there wouldn't be much in the way of conversation from Rick. He'd been writing before the intrusion, and it had been going well, beautifully and mechanically, in the sense that he appeared to have found his stride and his style, which meant no style, but simply to put it down as it came, and it did keep coming.

"You some kind of Shakespeare or something?"

Rick had wanted to ask him how it was that he had a key to Iris' house. But that would be more conversation and too much information.

"Not quite."

Chuck started to turn on the TV, but a glance from Rick told him not to, and Rick was surprised at this touch of sensitivity.

"I read, you know."

Rick stared at this laptop, would pretend to be writing, only to be left alone.

"Good."

"Yeah, but I'm not big on Shakespeare."

How fascinating, thought Rick.

"You read the Bible?"

Silence wasn't helping, so Rick said, "Yes."

"Do you believe in God?"

"Only when he's around and helps out."

"Hah. I know what you mean. Who do you like?"

He'd have to put a stop to this, but he replied, "So far as what?"

"Well I don't mean farmers. I mean writers."

"Some I like. Some I don't."

"I know what you mean. Me, I like that guy Montaigne."

Now that was something from leftfield, and for that reason Rick wasn't sure he had heard correctly. Montaigne was one of Rick's favorites.

"Who?"

"You never heard of Michel de Montaigne?"

"Oh that guy," said Rick. "Sure."

"I figured you did. I guess she's staying late. I forgot this is her night at the library."

So he knew her well enough to know that and what else?

"They're having a short story contest going on," Rick explained. "That must be the reason."

Chuck still did not move and now Rick wondered, without worrying, what might come next.

The man did not appear to be dangerous. At first, yes.

"Montaigne wrote short stories," Chuck said.

Okay, thought Rick. I guess this goes on.

"Essays, really," Rick said.

"Which one's your favorite?"

"Tough to choose."

"I like the one about noble savages and how primitives out in the wild, so-called, are more civilized than people who think they're so civilized."

"The one that's called something like 'Christians and Cannibals' is the one I think you mean."

"Hey, right," said Chuck.

He got up, stretched and left, saying, "Just tell her Chuck was here and I'll catch her next time."

"Will do."

* * * * *

He did.

He told her everything that he remembered about Chuck, the man who had broken the harmony of the household.

The man who had broken the deal, the deal about nothing coming between them, the deal that would let him work and live sheltered.

He told her about the topics that had come up, the Bible, God, Montaigne and – and what was that all about?

He told her about the racket from the motorcycle that broke the peace of the woods and the neighborhood, and about the chains and tattoos.

He told her that if there would be a second time he would move out and move into a motel.

He told her that before the interruption he'd been in the middle of a crucial chapter, now lost.

"I'm so sorry," she said. "So terribly sorry."

She ran to the bedroom and when she came out her eyes were swollen red.

"I don't need explanations," Rick said. "Only please..."

"We were married," she said flatly.

"I figured as much."

But there was much else he hadn't figured.

"Don't be fooled by his game. He teaches. He's tenured."

Dressed like that and talking like that – these days, yes.

"He puts it on, plays that game of being an ignoramus, but he is a genius and he does teach Montaigne," Iris explained.

"Where?"

"At the community college up the road. They wouldn't take him at Princeton or Harvard, where he belongs. He doesn't, you know, fit."

Rick stopped her right there to make a dash to his laptop to get that down, the revelation about Chuck and so much besides, and Iris wasn't sure what she had said that was so special, but to Rick it was extraordinary, that line, that phrase – "He doesn't, you know, fit."

He'd never heard it summed up so perfectly, so poetically, yes poetically: "He doesn't, you know, fit."

That could be said for the lives of so many men.

"He doesn't, you know, fit."

That defined a universe. For Rick it did.

He turned it over and how it would sound differently and not nearly as powerfully if she had pronounced it as – "He doesn't fit, you know."

No, that didn't do a thing. That way it had no punch. But this way it walloped: "He doesn't, you know, fit."

This way it moved like a psalm, like prayer. The message was universal, and the message was personal, very personal.

Rick now had the theme that had been eluding him, in those words the grounding for his entire novel.

The fictitious but true story, too true, about a man who does not, you know, fit.

* * * * *

Iris told him the story, but Rick knew such stories and he kept trying to make her stop, but she wanted him to know, and he knew.

He knew it from her and he knew it from himself and from everybody else. Life is tough. Life is complicated. Life is misery. But we go on.

That's where it was different with Chuck...Chuck and his drinking, his drugs and his suicidal tendencies. He kept wanting it to end.

Rick had heard all that before, too.

So she could not take it anymore.

He'd heard that, too.

But they were still friends.

That too he had heard a thousand times.

"He had no right to just show up," she said, no longer tearful, but regretful.

"But you did tell him about me."

"I had to, Rick, to warn him against any surprise visits."

"So he was just checking me out."

"I think so."

"Worried about your safety?"

"I think so," Iris said.

"Worried about your bringing in strays?" Rick said with an honest smile and laugh.

"You're my beautiful stray," she said falling into his arms.

* * * * *

So that's how it is, he was thinking as he walked along the woods with his cane, talking to himself. There are no accidents. There are no coincidences. All of it is for a purpose, all of it is to the good. All of it is part of a plan, God knows what! A man loves a woman and marries her and she destroys him but this too is all to the good.

A career in shambles, cars ending up in ditches, strangers appearing from out of nowhere, that too is part of a plan.

There may be no such thing as free will and if so, go along for the ride and quit feeling sorry for yourself and quit bitching.

It's all been decided beforehand, and if not, it's still the same trip. Feel the pain, yes, but without regrets and without vengeance.

Chapter 12

"Yes, I still do have connections. I do have some pull," Ruben was telling Marjorie at Bouley for a big and very expensive dinner.

She looked more glamorous than ever, though restless because the subject of London troubled her, made her feel like a woman on the make.

Made her feel like she was using him, which was true but only half the story. She really did love him.

Then there was Rick out there, somewhere, and she felt a strong attachment for him too, even love, but she still had not heard back.

Once, yes, that he was with old friends and needed the time off. That made sense. That she understood. But that was months ago.

Was he writing? Had he given up? Was he trying something new? He wouldn't say. Was he taking care of himself? Was he happy? Same answer.

Was he down in the dumps? This is what worried her.

They'd stopped talking about him, as though it had become taboo, but she still thought about him, and cared.

"Good," she said, distracted, there at the most expensive restaurant in New York.

"Good?"

"Well what more do you want me to say?"

The most important topic of her life and what a strange attitude.

"Maybe you should put down that drink," Ruben suggested.

"Maybe I shouldn't. Maybe men should stop telling me what I should and should not do."

So that's the way it is, thought Ruben. The other Marjorie. The evil twin. Not what he had expected for a $12,000 dinner tab.

Expensive place. Well, expensive woman. Oh yes. No trifling with this princess for any amount of money.

In England they called it "being in a mood" when royalty acted in a snit. So this was royalty and this was a snit.

He could tell that no amount of charm would get her out of this mood.

"So," she was saying, gazing about the room, "tell me what more you can do for me."

"I never said that there was anything I can do, Marjorie."

"So why did you bring me here, to talk about what?"

"Your next move, or so I thought."

"Oh that's right."

"I was saying that I could and would give it my best shot."

"I'd be so terribly grateful," she said sarcastically and with a British accent.

This is where it would be different if the person sitting across from him were a man. Then he'd know what to do. He'd take him outside. He'd taken many of them outside and when it was all over he was the only one left standing. So simple. Among men, so simple.

This I do not need, he was thinking. I don't need the money. I would take no money if only for the satisfaction of doing the work.

Journalism was sacred to Ruben Franklin and therefore the nonsense was sacrilegious.

"Will it be like this all night?" he asked her.

"Depends."

"On what?"

"It's gotten awfully stuffy in here," she said. "Is there no air conditioning?"

"Depends on what, Marjorie?"

"Depends on your ability to entertain me."

He could get up and leave and it was a thought to consider, along with tossing the wine across her glorious puss. He could do this and as he sat there studying her he played with the notion of quitting the moment he returned to the newsroom where it would be a pleasure to wave them all goodbye.

Then he'd retire to his villas. He had them everywhere. God, his family had done well, so well that he never really knew how much he was worth, and it could be hundreds of millions. He had people who took care of that part as he had people who took care of everything.

He knew how lucky he was from birth onward. Damn lucky. He never forgot his good fortune, with his good looks tossed in for a bonus.

He could have spent it all on leisure. But he needed work and as corny as it sounded to him, he owed the world some form of return for his blessings.

He had found soldiering and he had found journalism and he had found America and he had found Marjorie Carmen.

This one was something. There'd been others. But this one was something all right, blissfully American down to her toes and how she ruled, as Hemingway had remarked about a previous generation of American female bitchery, but now, in this generation, ruled double-time when they got the upper hand and had rights, those rights codified by law, that their mothers never dreamed of even as they marched.

They earned what they got, give them that, but how they lorded it over their men when they got the chance.

How smoothly they could turn from sweetness to nastiness once they reached that level of success.

Did they know that in more than three quarters of the world their sisters had no chance, no chances at all?

If they knew, did they care?

So did they know and did they care that in those countries where he had fought he found women enslaved? Millions of them. No, billions.

Did they know how lucky and how spoiled and how pampered they were to have been born in the right place at the right time?

Tell them and they'd scoff. They'd blame it on men, and they'd be right, but they'd be wrong on American men, men who'd surrounded their balls.

So it was sisters unite in America. The clit was their weapon.

He'll try. She certainly was worth a try.

"What hurts, Marjorie?"

"I don't like getting pushed around, if you must know."

"You can say that to me?"

She yawned. She waved back to a few people. She took a sip. Put it down.

"You seem to be really enjoying that steak," she said, irritably.

"Excuse me?"

"You must be famished, poor dear."

Now he knew something was wrong.

"About your getting pushed around..."

She took a few more sips, ignoring the comment, to suggest she had other things on her mind, and that the least of it was Ruben Franklin.

"What did you say?"

"You heard me."

"Nobody likes getting pushed around," she said, getting more irritated and testy.

"You mean the newsroom?"

"Oh, the newsroom and everything."

"Names? You want to mention names?"

"I thought you're moving me to the BBC," she said. "Isn't that why we're here, along with you and your steak?"

Something about his enjoying his food was certainly annoying her. This was a new one. Used to be she could eat him under the table.

"I said I'll do what I can. You deserve the chance."

She laughed and it was not a pleasant laugh. "Who do you know over there, the Queen?"

"You're being unkind, Marjorie, but yes, I've met the Queen. In fact..."

"Do I have to hear this?"

Yes, she did, and he told her how generations ago his people had loaned money to the Queen's people.

"I'm impressed," she said unimpressed.

He felt foolish. It certainly was foolish and futile trying to score points that way, through family connections she could never comprehend. She would never understand what it was like to be part of a dynasty that was so wealthy, so glorious and so generous but that still, as his grandfather used to complain, finds itself on the run at the whim of the wrong tyrant.

Worth billions, bankers to kings, but still refugees. His father got the family out of France in the nick of time when Hitler came to power.

Everything that was confiscated, throughout Europe, had to be restored, and was restored.

The family knew how to build, but generation after generation, heirs had to learn how to rebuild.

His father used to say, "They'll never leave us alone," and his father had been knighted.

The thoroughbred breeding operation was Ruben's own contribution to the dynasty.

"I should not need to impress you," he shot back now finding his own aristocratic backbone.

How, he now asked himself, would an American woman so insulated and so indulged compete in a world that was so different, if somehow he could get her a shot at the snobbish BBC? He knew her and he knew them over there and it might work, but the chances were slim.

Her American stardom would count against her. They'd show her what it means to be uppity.

They'd educate her on keeping it low key and teach her that around here we don't go for "be yourself."

Be British was the only style. Her hair, her make-up, her wardrobe, her brashness, her diction – they'd make her start from scratch.

"Is that all we're going to do is eat and drink?" she said.

"No, but I've already made a few calls, and there is some interest."

But Marjorie didn't seem interested.

"You'll have to tell me about it someday."

"Why not now?"

"Well you're so busy eating," she said with a scornful laugh.

"Do you mind?"

"Do whatever you want, Ruben. Are you going to have dessert?"

"You're not?"

She had only been picking at her steak, eyes all over the room.

"I'm not that hungry."

"So I've noticed."

"You're doing well enough for the both of us," she said.

"What's wrong, Marjorie?"

"Nothing's wrong. I just don't feel like eating, or talking. So what did you say to the BBC?"

"I'm not sure this is the right time to tell you, not in that mood."

"I'm not their cup of tea, right?"

That wasn't true, only Ruben was getting himself into a mood. He had not bargained for this, a snooty Marjorie Carmen.

Had she ever been like this before?

Nothing that he could remember. She'd had her flare-ups but temperament was expected in the heated climate of the newsroom.

Together as lovers there'd always been heat, but of a different kind and he resented being the target of whatever it was that was troubling her.

She got up, where everyone ogled her and whispered, mostly in approval, and went to the bathroom, and came back with fresh make-up.

Also a fresh attitude.

"Oh," she said, putting on a show of being nonchalant, "I guess I'm just in a slump."

That could be it, he agreed.

"We all go through slumps, Ruben, don't you think?"

"Yes, we do."

Now for the kill, and she was not smiling: "Except for Carla!"

So was that it, what this was all about? Carla Bruin was her main rival, almost as big as Marjorie, almost as beautiful, almost as powerful over the airwaves, almost as admired inside and outside the newsroom, almost as glamorous – almost everything but never quite enough. Carla was the type who would always be second best, fated by chance to be runner-up.

But for the upcoming White House Correspondents' Dinner, this time, this one time, Carla Bruin had come in first.

She was the one chosen to represent the network at the festivities. A plum get.

Obviously, Marjorie's disastrous hour with the President was still paying unwanted dividends.

So this was the cause of her gloom. This? Had to be.

"Marjorie, don't tell me you're jealous?"

She was on fire.

"Just tell me who made the decision."

Aha, the decision to choose Carla Bruin over Marjorie Carmen for this one event, a big event, yes – prestigious.

This was where it was proved Who was Who in the trade – who was in, who was out, and seemingly Marjorie was out.

This was not supposed to happen. But Carla deserved the shot and overall posed no threat to Marjorie.

Go tell that to Marjorie, who was steamed.

"We all did."

"You all made the decision? That's a cop-out. You're better than that, Ruben. Who made the decision? I won't tell. I'll be a good girl."

"No you won't."

"Hah. Come on, Ruben. Spill the beans."

Well, what to tell, because both Ruben and Russ Appleton knew there'd be hell to pay either way with two clashing divas, and Russ kept saying that it ought to be Carla's turn and besides...yes, besides Marjorie finding herself on the President's enemies' list, or hate list as people said about a President who knew how to keep a grudge.

To have her show up would be rubbing it in, as Russ had it figured – and Ruben likewise.

She was sure to be unwelcome, snubbed, and cause for gossip. Best to let her wait for next year when she'd likely be out of the White House doghouse.

For the good of the network, best to keep Marjorie under wraps for an event that would play on for days and weeks.

We don't need another black eye.

Ruben agreed, but there was still Marjorie to consider, Marjorie and how she might react.

Fireworks, to be sure.

She would not take this well.

Hell, no, and hell hath no fury like Marjorie Carmen scorned.

But this is business.

So it was agreed and it was unanimous.

"I take full responsibility," Ruben said, adding to the clichés that were so common in the trade.

"Well, at least you're being honest, since you weren't being chivalrous."

She kept glaring at him.

He was prepared to say that it wasn't about her; it was about Carla and giving everyone at the network an even chance.

But she'd know it for the bullshit that it was, because it was about her. The entire network was about her, or getting to be so anyway.

"I could have blamed Russ," he said.

"Oh – I don't want to talk about Russ."

She took another sip. Dabbed her lips.

"You feel neglected?"

"I feel bored."

"Bored."

"Yes, bored, Ruben."

"With what?"

"With everything."

"That's not true. You're still tops..."

"Oh who cares," she sighed as if she really didn't care.

Ruben finished his steak and ordered coffee and dessert. She'll have the coffee but declined dessert.

"You really came here to eat," she taunted.

"That's why we call these places restaurants."

"I've just never seen you enjoy your food so much. Usually when we go out..."

He was beginning to take the hint. How stupid of him to have missed it all evening. All of this could have been avoided.

"Marjorie."

"Yes."

"You're not bored."

"Yes, I am."

"Marjorie Carmen is not bored," he teased, making it a game.

"Marjorie Carmen is bored," she played along.

"I'll tell you what Marjorie wants."

"Hah," she laughed.

Then he moved across the table and whispered, "Marjorie wants to get laid."

She didn't respond but turned red, a pleasant red, a very pleasant red.

"Marjorie Carmen," Ruben went on back at his seat, "wants to get laid right now. That's what this is all about."

She smiled, the first true smile of the evening, and she blushed.

"Marjorie Carmen," Ruben went on, "wants no foreplay."

"She may have just had it," she agreed, flushed.

"Marjorie Carmen wants to be taken to the apartment right now and get herself laid right now."

"Will she?" she asked.

She did.

* * * * *

That same night, after all that and more, men came to visit and it was about a motel owner, Leroy Larson, who'd been found dead.

He'd been murdered in room 601.

There was a suspicion that a particular man who had signed in and was assigned to that room was in fact Ruben Franklin.

Along with someone nationally famous, a woman.

Would Ruben know anything about this?

No, nothing.

A son, a son of Mr. Larson's, Clyde, had reported the homicide and was himself under suspicion.

Did Ruben know anything about that – and only asking?

No, nothing.

But a particular license plate recorded at the motel matched an automobile belonging to Ruben Franklin.

Did he have an explanation?

Strange, said Ruben, but he had no explanation.

Good enough, said the men, for now.

The investigation continues.

* * * * *

Later she asked him if there was anything to worry about and he said no, nothing happened.

But something did happen.

Nothing to worry about.

She liked that about Ruben, the certainty about his convictions. She loved that about him.

But something did happen.

"I'll take care of everything," he said.

In fact he already had.

She'd rather not know. So she did not ask and he did not tell. He wouldn't tell her even if she asked, and she knew better than to ask.

He told her that there was a world of men that women knew nothing about, and best to keep it that way.

"That's terrible," she said. "When was that? What century?"

Every century, he explained, and no amount of new rules would ever change human nature.

Men traded signals among themselves…and it was no different with women.

"We've advanced far beyond that," she insisted.

"Not as much as you think."

She considered pursuing the argument, but for some reason she was pleased. It's what made him Ruben Franklin.

Chapter 13

The Wilderness Years. That was the book everybody was reading. Not the one by Churchill. This one was written by Rick Callow under the name Rick Code. Rick had given this some serious thought, about going pseudonym, especially after his publisher, Mimi Zilber, who also served as his editor, flipped for the book, guaranteed gargantuan sales, and to prove it began with a run of 500,000 copies, which sold out in 11 days, not counting online sales.

There were more runs coming, but never enough to keep up.

He'd be famous as Rick Callow, who was known in some circles, but he chose Rick Code, who was known nowhere, until now.

Now, as Rick Code, he was the most famous writer in America and in many parts around the world, and it meant nothing to him.

Neither did it mean a thing to Iris at home or to Marjorie Carmen in New York, or to anybody in New York. Marjorie did not know the name. Or the man.

To Iris he was still Rick who had finished a book and had taken it to New York, beard and all, plus jeans and a cane and no haircut, and had or had not succeeded in getting it published. He would not say because it would not matter and for weeks, after he had given the book its final period, he reflected on keeping it unpublished.

He had no need for glory, but money was running low. If somehow he could get it published without sensation, that would be okay, and so the new name was a simple move, but he was still not happy about it leaving his hands. He had fallen in love with it, not because it was so great, though maybe it was, but because he knew that it could never get as good for him ever again.

He had not written *the* perfect novel, but he had written *his* perfect novel, and something about this was terrifying, something like death.

He'd never be able to exceed. There'd be no follow-up, no sequel, no more typing. This was terrible to consider.

He was doomed with a bestseller.

The title had been the brainchild of his editor, Mimi, who had seen in the book something near biblical, a wanderer in search of a promised land or a promised life, always in the distance but never attained, always within reach following the next mirage.

She saw in it everyman's search for the jackpot only to find more wilderness. There was no getting out. The search was everything.

She also saw in it a man with a broken heart.

He met with her three times in New York, only because he had to, and there would be no big-time editor-to-writer dinners for the launch of a big book. He did not want that and she understood and he wanted no publicity about himself either, and she understood this, too.

He wanted nothing, really. He still loved the town, but it was his town no more. It was Marjorie's town. He had no urge to see her. Not yet.

Someday. Maybe.

Meantime he was done with that fast crowd. He'd had his dose and his fill.

On that day there would be not much to say. The kids were not his. He'd been a good stepfather to them, but had never felt necessary. They had their nannies. They had their mother, and they had their real father. So he was not necessary then and he was not necessary now.

He still refused to watch television, except for the movies, and when he did, when he caught a moment of news he found that still nothing had changed, and when he caught Marjorie on the Alpha News network, he found that she too had not changed, except to be more beautiful than ever, and it hurt, it did hurt, but not as much as before.

Sometimes it hurt more than before, mostly after a few drinks or on first getting up in the morning when everything hurt, all the memories.

But the memories, about all of them, he'd already made good riddance through the book.

He had not told all. He had told it in code and that was how he came by the name, Rick Code.

He did not write trash. He had trashed nobody. On that score he was absolutely satisfied. His first two books were also not trash, but not good enough, but that was when he'd been Rick Callow and had written what he thought they wanted and that, that was trash, a trashy way to write.

This time he had written what he wanted and this was the result. Through his editor, invitations came in to have him give lectures at Columbia, Harvard, Princeton and other places of high learning. He declined, and he declined offers to appear on radio and television. He did not tweet. He did not blog. He had no face on Facebook. He was offered honorary degrees, chairs, and chances to teach anywhere and he declined everything.

People wanted him to read their manuscripts and to this he agreed and then stopped because to this there would be no end...and in the end they all got petulant and resentful when he couldn't get them published. He found it safer to ignore any and all requests.

So many writers, everyone with a book, every one of them hungry for recognition – and big bucks. What to do with all these writers?

Was there anyone left who wasn't writing a book?

Hollywood phoned. Mimi asked him to take the call. He did, for the sake of the publishing house and what it could do for business.

"Give in just this much," Mimi pleaded.

About a movie, he was still undecided, but if Mimi insisted he would have to give in, but no public appearances for him and no publicity for him.

But he owed her allegiance. An editor with an understanding heart was a rarity.

Hollywood kept calling and he'd already heard smart, fast-talking voices on the phone with offers up to the sky. That was before. But this time he knew they would make good, not like the other two times, no those other two times the hypocrisy ran thick. He'd been a soft touch, a sap, a sucker for their big dreams and false promises.

As Rick Code it would be different.

"This meeting you have to attend," Mimi said, and because it was Mimi, he attended.

These were the money boys. The preliminaries had been done and the green light had come fast and straight from the top.

The name Rick Code meant something.

Now he found himself in Los Angeles for more talk, maybe final talk, about a movie. He walked in and nearly a dozen of them nearly bowed when he made his entrance. The head of the studio brought him coffee. Everyone smiled and waited for him to speak. He preferred to listen.

They talked big actors, big directors, big money. He listened. They kept asking him what he thought. He said, "I'm listening."

The head of the studio stepped out and brought back a bag of donuts, all for him. She'd been told, by Mimi, that he liked them glazed.

He knew none of these people and they only knew him as Rick Code. There was one exception. The man he knew was Edward Blatt, but he was not sure, though quite sure that this was the producer that had at one time made a fool of him, and in front of a big crowd that included friends and family.

* * * * *

That, in the past, was in New York when his first book came out, and there was all that hope and hoopla and Marjorie had pushed it over the air, which she'd been reluctant to do because it made the entire scene so obvious – winning wife gives loser husband a helping hand.

Something about it gave her the creeps, and her tech crew squirmed when she held up the book. Rick hadn't asked for the favor, but he wanted it, just like everybody else who wanted a mention on her show, and then there was Matt Owens, the biggest anchorman of them all who pimped his own books every night on the air, books he'd never written himself.

Well no one could say that about Rick Callow's book. Every word of it in there was his, and now the fanfare! A sure winner, everybody said, and with Marjorie and the entire Alpha News team at his side, can't lose. They made a gala for him at the Warwick and everybody showed up and made long windy speeches.

When it came to Rick, good old Rick, pathetic Rick, husband to Marjorie Carmen but on the move to make a big splash for himself, there wasn't much time left to speak. He was the keynote speaker. He had spent weeks honing every word. This was to be the biggest speech of his life.

This was where he would prove them all wrong, that he wasn't an empty suit living off the triumphs that belonged to his wife.

There was plenty of that going around, but now he had the chance to show that he was no leech...show them all.

But the lights started going down. The room had been booked for the next party. He was supposed to have 20 minutes.

Five minutes were left. Maybe 10 if he talked fast. Ridiculous, but he began...and as soon as he began the man next to him began elbowing him and urging him to speed it up, which got Rick too flustered to make any sense, and people began laughing where they weren't supposed to laugh.

"Hurry it up, kid," the man said in a booming voice. "People want dessert and the coffee's getting cold."

Rick tore up his prepared remarks and stomped off.

Who was that man?

* * * * *

Now, in the middle of all the big talk, Rick, now Rick Code, held up an arm and everything stopped. He turned to the man who might be Ed Blatt.

"Excuse me. But we haven't been properly introduced."

"I'm Edward Blatt and come to think of it, don't I know you from somewhere?"

Rick nodded.

"I thought so."

The head of the studio apologized for her failure to introduce everyone properly. She began...

"No need," said Rick. "But how does this Blatt fit into the picture?"

"Oh he's executive producer."

"Can he be replaced?"

"Excuse me?"

"Can his butt get kicked out of here?"

They huddled.

"Is there a problem?"

"Yes, it's him or me."

Without Rick there was no movie.

"But he's in the contract. He wrote the contract. He's the lawyer."

"So he stays?"

"We don't know what this is all about, Mr. Code, but can this be discussed, negotiated?"

"I'm sick to my stomach just to be in the same room with that son of a bitch. He's in. I'm out."

Mimi chased after him, but it was no use.

* * * * *

Rick stopped over at the library a few times. Iris worked there part time, two nights a week, and he'd stopped being amazed at what he saw.

The place was piled high with his books and as fast as they came in they were checked out. There was a section named specially for Rick Code.

Nobody knew he was Rick Code. The book carried no picture of him. That was the deal he'd made with Mimi Zilber.

He liked to browse and sometimes he took a chair, way in back, when the library's Reading Club discussed a particular book.

One day that particular book was Rick Code's *The Wilderness Years*.

"You can't miss that," Iris said.

"Yes, I can."

But she persuaded him.

So there he was, incognito, listening to them talk about a book he never wrote. Well it was his book all right, but everybody read it differently.

They all saw it from different angles, angles he'd never imagined.

"The writer," he whispered to Iris, "is the last to know."

They all brought their own life's experiences into a book somebody else wrote, and this, Rick decided, was a good thing.

Sometimes the talk got snippy, even hostile. They all wanted to know what the writer really meant and for Rick this was an excellent question.

Even the writer doesn't know what he really means so he keeps on writing to find out.

Iris kept wanting him to reveal himself, for once, but that was not going to happen.

They liked the book, some, most, loved the book, but of the 20 in the room, two dissented.

Well, he thought, there are always those and that's the chance you take. This was like a jury.

Guilty or innocent... The human condition was all about awaiting the verdict.

"Keep in mind," he said, "when you have a book in your hands, you have the writer's life in your hands."

But he did not say it loudly enough for anyone to hear.

Someone said how incredible it was to write a book. You must be a genius, and Rick remembered the auto mechanic saying the same thing. "You're a writer? You must be a genius," saying it as he was taking apart an entire transmission bolt by bolt. Well that too is genius. We are all geniuses at something. The trick is to find out what it is.

One day he agreed to go to a reading to be given by a New York author. The man read and it was quite boring. The applause was polite.

Then he answered questions and Rick felt sorry for him, even though this guy was big time, not as big as Rick Code, nobody was as big as Rick Code these days, but major league, this guy, but he wasn't connecting, not for Rick. He was too professorial.

He was talking down to the people, as New Yorkers often do when they are in another town.

You can't explain a book, just like you can't explain yourself.

Often in the past he resented other books and other writers, but now he did not care. He was doing all right.

* * * * *

Then she persuaded him to answer a few questions for the local radio station, and he consented on condition that it remain local.

He'd refuse if there were any chance of it getting broadcast wide, and so it was agreed.

"Writing is holy."

"I'm not sure what that means," said the host.

"I'm not sure, either."

"Are you suggesting something mystical?"

"Something happens."

"Something mystical," the host persisted.

"If you mean do I hear voices, no I don't."

"So something..."

"Yes, something comes from another dimension. Call it a parallel universe, if you like."

"Do you consider yourself an artist?"

"Everybody's an artist. The carpenter is an artist and so is the plumber. We all just do it differently."

"There's quite a bit of sex in your book."

"There's also plenty of it in life. It's been going around, and came around even before I arrived on the scene."

"Can you tell us something about yourself... where you were born..."

"No, I can't."

"People know nothing about you. Are you happy with that?"

"Delighted."

"What time of day is best for you to write?"

"The morning."

"Any reason why?"

"Could be because the subconscious has been piling up overnight."

"Are you married?"

"Next question, please."

The deal had been no personal questions.

"What are your plans for your next book?"

Dead air, so the host repeated the question.

"There won't be a next book."

"That's surprising."

"Yes."

"But isn't it strange?"

"Yes."

"Is it that you feel you've said it all?"

"No. Nobody says it all. We just say what we have to say."

"So for you, you feel you're done as a writer?"

"I wouldn't put it quite that way. But for me, I'm done."

"That is sure to disappoint a lot of readers."

"They'll manage."

"You have millions of fans."

"I haven't been counting."

"How does it feel to have written such a smash?"
"Feels fine."
"You seem to have come from out of nowhere."
"Exactly."
"Do you answer fan mail?"
"No."
"I guess that would take up too much time."
"That's one reason."
"Some fans and reporters who've visited your compound and spoken to your neighbors report that you frequently walk the woods talking to yourself."

True, these fans kept coming from around the country and around the world. Stalkers started coming around.

"Must be somebody else."
"This person they say has a long beard, walks with a cane and gives the appearance of a prophet."
"You can be sure that is somebody else."
"But you are something of a hermit."
"Next question."
"Can we get back to the first question, about what you said?"
"What did I say?"
"About writing being holy."

* * * * *

That did it all right, and promises were not kept. The interview was broadcast nationally and around the globe.

People misunderstood, as he knew they would. What does it mean!

Were these words of wisdom from a great man, the world's most famous reclusive author, or the rantings from an eccentric?

Sales of the book zoomed higher and higher.

Chapter 14

She'd become more edgy and argumentative with the guests on her show, and Russ Appleton wanted to know if this was some sort of lease breaking deal going on, and then there'd been those phone calls to him from London, the old boy network in action about her making other plans.

Was Ruben aware of this?

More than that, Ruben admitted, "I put her in touch with some of my connections."

"So you're helping her leave?"

"No, I'm helping her do what she wants to do and whatever Marjorie wants, Marjorie gets, and nobody is going to stop her."

Better, Ruben argued, to stay on her good side.

Russ had no choice but to agree that to fight her would only make her more contrary and spiteful enough to quit on those grounds alone.

That part of it was understandable to Russ, but the other part wasn't, the part where Ruben was being an accomplice.

Ruben knew that he could get fired on the spot, but he also knew that he had ten times more money than Russ.

He didn't need this job or any job. He did it because it was his duty to journalism, and this was where fate had planted him.

Fate may have other plans for him, too.

"Since you brought it up, Russ, I must say you haven't been quite fatherly to her...as of late."

"I created her!"

That he did.

"You've been harsh and unforgiving about that one screw-up."

"I agree. I told you before I agree, and you said you would straighten it out. I did not expect you to straighten it out this way."

"Nothing is for keeps in this business, I don't have to tell you."

* * * * *

"I'm not being a good girl?" she teased.

They were driving to meet the highest exec stationed here from London.

"He's afraid of losing you."

"He ought to be."

She started going on about all the others in the newsroom who were conspiring against her.

"You never used to be this way, Marjorie."

"Oh, I'm starting to sound paranoid, am I?"

"Yes."

"But I could still be right."

"True," he laughed.

They stopped at a diner. The waitress took their order without a second look.

"Hmmm," Marjorie said.

"What?"

"Not the usual."

She meant the attention she usually got. But this wasn't skyscraper America. This was grassroots America.

No one else in the diner was smitten.

"Not everybody's hooked on the news, Marjorie. Alpha News is just another click of the dial."

She didn't say anything.

"You seem shocked."

"I guess I am."

"I think we're all in for a big surprise when we realize that we're not so special, that Americans have other things on their minds."

"Besides us," Marjorie agreed, reluctantly.

"So this is a revelation?"

"It is an eye-opener, Ruben. It is."

There was more of it to come.

*****

The exec's name was Hiram Giddings. Ruben knew him, but not too well.

"My," he said, "you are more beautiful in person."

"Thank you."

"So, Ruben, this is the big secret you've been keeping."

"No secret," Ruben said, "to the twelve million viewers who watch her every night."

"Touché."

Hiram wanted to know precisely what she had in mind. She was ready for this.

"To bring a touch of America to your worldwide audience," she replied, satisfied that she got it down as rehearsed.

Ruben had warned her to watch her words, to remember that in this instance she was the supplicant.

"You feel we're lacking?" Hiram challenged.

Think fast.

"No. Well, yes."

"Yes and no?"

"You do give us coverage, but only when something breaks."

"What else should it be?"

"There's nothing about us...about our advances... about our culture."

"You mean we still treat you as the poor cousin in the family of the world."

"I'll answer that," said Ruben. "Yes."

"Do you agree?" Hiram turned to Marjorie.

"Something like that," she said.

"Like what?"

"Like...well like we're just an incidental part of the world."

"But you think America is something special."

"Yes, I do."

"You think Americans are better."

"She never said that," Ruben rushed in.

"I never would."

Hiram sat back and seemed to enjoy watching them squirm.

"Are you aware that in much of the world the United States is detested?"

"I did not intend to go into all that," Marjorie put in strong and straight. "That's a separate discussion."

"Are you aware that for all your advances, you still have race…"

"You still have anti-Semitism," Ruben charged in.

"Race and other problems," the man from London continued.

"This isn't what I had in mind," said Marjorie.

"I'm sure it isn't."

"Easy now, Hiram," Ruben warned.

"No," Hiram continued, "you thought we'd jump at the chance to teach us how it's done when we taught you."

This was an opening for something rhetorical.

"We're not talking about the times the United States had to come rescue Europe from devouring itself, are we, Hiram."

"That's fair, Ruben. But you, Miss Carmen…"

"You can call me Marjorie."

"I fear, Marjorie, for all your fame and glory in the United States, you may be out of step, or out of your depth, for our European viewers and the larger world."

"Now that's not fair," she stiffened. "I'm not looking to change the world, only to report."

"But you do commentary."

"Yes, and I think you can use more flair in that department."

"Granted, you do have flair – but would it translate?"

"I don't see why not?" said Ruben.

"We do speak the same language," she said, "last time I checked."

"No we don't. We have a particular world view."

"Certainly nothing American to that view," Ruben piped in.

"Precisely."

"So be precise," said Marjorie.

"To put it to you straight, the world according to us views the United States as a bully."

"Not counting," Marjorie replied sharply, "that we're the first ones to rush in whenever there's a catastrophe."

"You do come calling," added Ruben.

"Can we get back to journalism?" Marjorie urged.

"Yes, so let's just say that your journalism is not our journalism. Does that suffice as an answer?"

"Stiff upper lip," she said.

"More or less. Would you know how to address the Queen?"

"This is ridiculous. I'm sorry we took up your time," Marjorie said, getting up.

"No, wait. Please wait. Let's call this a test to see how far I could push you in case you thought we'd be so thrilled to have you teach us the American way."

"As if the European way has done wonders," snapped Marjorie.

"I must say, your choice of Presidents does leave much to be desired."

"But we've never managed a Mussolini or a Hitler," said Ruben.

"Thank you for your time," said Marjorie.

"You are welcome, and I will bring you up in London. I think you'll do."

* * * * *

"UGGGHHH," she howled back in the car.

"So now you know."

"The arrogance! The supercilious highhanded arrogance! Are they all like that?"

"No, we just caught the wrong fish."

"What did he mean I'll do?"

"He meant you passed the test and that he will recommend you."

"It's no sure thing on my part."

"I intended for something like this to give you a sharp kick in the butt."

"Was that your plan? To sour my appetite?"

"Not entirely."

"Did you hear that man?"

"Yes, Marjorie. I heard that man."

"Out of my depth! What else did he say, that awful man?"

"Let me think."

"Out of step," Marjorie remembered.

"That was a good one."

"That son of a bitch."

"That's my girl."

"After something like that, you know what I feel like saying? I feel like saying, God bless America. How corny. But there comes a time to be corny."

"All you need is a touch of the rest of the world."

"You've been right all along, Ruben. We are parochial, and I'm glad of it, if you don't mind."

They drove without speaking.

Then she said, "After something like that, you know what I feel like doing?" And they did.

* * * * *

Now she'd begun worrying about losing her shine with her public. Her ratings were still okay. The numbers were holding, but weren't improving, either. In fact there'd been something of a dip. Nothing to panic about. But she needed something to change. She had gotten tired of the same old routines and the usual guests.

She decided on an entirely new segment, which she called Poet's Corner, where writers and other thinkers could speak beyond sound bites. She had no trouble getting people. As expected, she'd energized the intellectual community, and publishers who'd been screaming for something like this, finally had a spot.

Writers who normally had to wait for C-Span to get more than three minutes of airtime, anywhere, were thrilled.

But it took time for her audience to get used to the switch. That crowd, mostly political, liked it hard and fast.

That audience was used to the back and forth, the smack down and the put down, and they liked to cheer or cheer this guest against that one.

That was how it went when politics ruled.

These new guests, artists, professors and writers were a breed that would take nursing, as would the audience.

People would have to get into the habit of listening to slowly developed reasoning, and some of these great minds knew how to drone on.

Marjorie was surprised to find that even some of the most popular writers around failed to draw.

There was one writer everybody wanted to hear. That was Rick Code.

But she had already tried and failed. She had sent out snoops, including private detectives to track him down, and they had, they'd found where he lived, but the place was surrounded by walls, fences, alarms, dogs and a private army, plus neighbors who refused to talk.

There were sightings about a man and his beard and his cane prowling the grounds deep in thought, and everything about him said keep away.

There was about him the air of a great man, not to be trifled.

* * * * *

Rick was finding it hard to have no writing to do and once in a while he was tempted to write just to keep busy. Iris was worried about him.

She wondered how long this would last, the two of them, because he needed her while he was at work on the book, but now not so much. He'd relied on her for reference material and simply to do the shopping and the cooking and to keep the household moving while he typed away.

Now he wasn't typing. Now he lounged about the house, restless, lost in thought. This can't end well, she worried.

She worried that he would leave her and the signs of it began in the bedroom where, now, he did not even try to perform.

She had bought new clothes, even went through a complete makeover at the salon to remain attractive to him. He didn't respond much.

He watched TV, the movies, and once in a while even the news.

* * * * *

"You shouldn't have said that," he told the TV, or rather to Marjorie on the TV, when she told a politician to stop talking "baloney."

He'd begun watching her studiously and concluding that, obvious perhaps to no one else, Marjorie was losing her style.

They had taken the starch out of her.

Her comebacks were still swift, and the sharp wit was still there, but coming with effort and not the usual ease...and then the temper.

Something must be going on, he thought, and not to the good, and it did not make him happy to see her struggling. He was rooting for her. He knew what it was like for her behind the scenes and how she'd had to fight for every promotion within a newsroom that pretended to be but never truly was on her side.

Every move had taken effort, and some guile, and there was no end to the sparring she had to do to stay on top or to just stay in the game. There was always somebody younger and hotter to take her spot and even those within her generation were always ready to move in. Anchorwoman sex appeal was no one's exclusive. America had them by the barrelful.

Newsroom intrigue was the same all over but at Alpha News it was different because they were mostly women vying for the same slots.

They were all blessed with brains, but the younger ones kept coming in with snazzier legs. That was half the battle.

A few moments here and there, he noticed, she lapsed into absentmindedness. Nobody else would notice this.

Then he noticed how quickly she grew irritable and how her face would begin to tighten and lose its delicious softness.

She was still beautiful but looking older.

He knew her well enough to catch the smile for a guest but the frown even before they went to commercial.

No one else would notice this. No one knew her as he did. Russ knew her. Ruben knew her. But not like he knew her.

"Snap out of it," he'd say, as if she could hear him.

He thought it was a great idea, the one about her Poet's Corner, and he was rooting for this too, and this too wasn't working. Great idea, but wrong audience, wrong time slot. Great idea, but the people she had on were just too intellectual and much too talkative and absolutely much too full of themselves.

"Make them shut up," he'd started yelling at the screen.

They all had books to sell and his own name came up quite often as the ultimate example of American literary success.

He got no pleasure from this, nor from the fact that this segment was losing, so far a dud. But he knew she'd persist to make it a winner.

Must have been some job to get that one approved. He could imagine her arguing that it was time for the network to show a touch of class.

Politics is killing the network as it's killing the country.

He could imagine Russ going on about how the network was built on politics...but Russ, Rick could hear her say, all the time?

All the damn time?
If it ain't broke...
Yeah...yeah...yeah...
Well this one's on you, sweetheart.
I'll take my chances.
But don't come crying to me if it flops.
Do I ever?

Doesn't she know that when she pulls her hair back like that, it makes her look severe? Doesn't Russ tell her these things? Where's Ruben to advise her? Or are they giving in to her to watch her fall flat on her face to make room for the next pair of legs, if they weren't grooming one already?

There were always more of these bright young hopefuls being cultivated in the farm system.

"Well I am no Rick Code," one of the authors submitted in a display of rare humility.

"You think he's that good?" quizzed Marjorie.

"Yes. What do you think?"

"I think he's great."

For a moment Rick felt like crying. How he'd craved that when he was Rick Callow, and for Rick Code the approval was genuine, as it had not been before.

He wondered if she'd read between the lines and perhaps knew that, hello, guess what?

No, he didn't think so, and of course he could straighten it all out by answering just one of her messages, but that he would not do, no never, or possibly never, because he'd made promises to himself and must not weaken to the temptation, and there had been temptation.

One phone call away from a most pleasant drama he could dream about, but to which he would never submit.

He'd worked too hard to make himself Rick Code. He had trained for it like a fighter. He'd read all the books to learn the different styles before he could find a style of writing to call is own, and only he could appreciate the miracle that came that certain day when he hit the keyboard.

Something happened that day, and kept on happening, which nobody would understand.

* * * * *

"Okay," he said when Iris told him she'd have to be gone for a few weeks to help out her ailing mother.

"You'll be all right?"

"I'll be all right."

She was worried. He was so absentminded. He couldn't do anything around the house, and about the house, they could have had a much bigger house. He had all the money in the world and even the neighbors, those who were in on the secret, wondered why he hadn't built a palace.

Well he had built some additions, but nothing grand, nothing to advertise that here lived the most famous author in the world.

Except, that is, for all the security he'd installed, and all the security people he'd hired.

He'd need a cook and someone to come do the dishes and the cleaning while she was gone, and she found someone from the library.

"You'll like Kathy," Iris said.

He knew Kathy from the library. She loved his book.

"Okay," he said.

He wasn't saying much more these days. He had his mind on something else altogether. Mimi Zilber, his editor, kept giving him the good news – great news about the numbers, record breaking, and he didn't care, and about the Pulitzer, and he didn't care, and about the Man Booker Prize, and he didn't care, perhaps the Nobel Prize, and he didn't care. He had his mind on Marjorie. He was obsessed.

* * * * *

He noticed that the lighting wasn't as good for her as it used to be, and then Carla Bruin subbing for her much too often, and then Greg Olman sitting in together with Marjorie as if co-hosting, only that one night, but a signal perhaps? What's next? What could possibly be next?

One bad inning and that's the game?

People don't know, they just don't know what it's like being in the public eye night after night, every night a new test, the bright lights shining on every flaw; the demand to always be perky and perfect. Pity?

For the girl who has everything? Nobody's asking for pity. Only for some understanding and to quit being hateful.

Too much of that going around.

Trip, and people used to laugh. Now they scorn, and for Marjorie the scorn kept coming.

Well he knew and damned well knew when it started; it started that lousy night with the President, the worst night of her career, and the chips still falling. All right, she'd goofed...but come on. Give the girl a break! This was so unfair, how they all kept piling on, and with such relish.

The snub against her for that big gala at the White House, he knew about that and that's when he wrote that op-ed in the *Times* defending her, and the editors at the *Times* had been so surprised to get something from Rick Code, who'd refused to come out of his shell even for them, even for the *Times*, refused a front page interview, that they had to get it okayed at the top to get it published on the chance that it might be fake. But the wording of the essay was so like the book that they figured it must be him, Rick Code, and Rick Code clinched it with a phone call from a throwaway cell phone.

Rick Callow, back then, they had written off for his "attempt at a vanity career as an author."

The Rick Code op-ed caused one hell of a stir and, weeks ago, got the buzz buzzing all over again.

Rick imagined it going like this back in the newsroom:

Russ Appleton: "Hey, Marjorie. How about this?"
Marjorie: "I know. I know."
Russ: "Do you know him?"
Marjorie: "Not a clue."
Russ: "Rick Code seems to know you. Sure does."
Marjorie: "Beats me."
Russ: "Well, we'll take it, anything from snob media. Not bad. Not bad at all."
Marjorie: "Glad you're happy, Russ. I'm here to please."
Russ: "No amount of money could pay for this kind of prestige. You're sure you don't know him?"
Marjorie: "Positively."
Russ: "I know you've been trying to get him."
Marjorie: "Everybody has. Biggest recluse on the planet."
Russ: "What a scoop that would be. How hard have you tried?"
Marjorie: "I've tried everything."
Russ: "I'll do what I can."

That was exactly how it went.

Chapter 15

"That bitch," Matt Owens was saying. "That ingrate, that bitch."

Matt had brought her along, as he had it figured, when she'd shared the morning spot with that kid whose name he kept forgetting. But he knew she was something, and brought it up with Ruben, that this girl ought to be moved up with a spot of her own. He'd give her a couple of minutes to shine on his own show, which got the biggest numbers of all, and that way introduce her to the network's prime time audience. Move her along slowly, but move her along.

That's how he remembered it and that's how he had it figured, and more than that, he's the one who first saw her when she was doing the news at that local station in Cincinnati and mentioned it to Russ, that here was somebody he should give a look – though about this he wasn't too sure, because Marjorie, on her own, had already applied for the job at Alpha News and had already gone through the interview process.

Anyway, he'd been her biggest booster and for some time her only booster, as he had it figured.

But they never showed gratitude, none of them, all of them that he'd helped bring up.

He didn't have to be so generous. But he was. That's just the way he was. Often, he reminded his viewers about his generosity.

He could never understand why around the newsroom and elsewhere around the network he wasn't so popular. He usually ate alone. Must be the jealousy and might even be fear. Can't be the arrogance because, as he always said to himself, in this business we are all prima donnas.

He even said so out loud when he met with his equals from the other networks and they all laughed and agreed, but did not like him, either.

Only the public liked him. The public did not love him. The public loved Marjorie Carmen and Marjorie Carmen was killing the network.

"That's a strong word," Ruben was saying.

Ruben never liked being in the same room with Matt Owens. When Matt was angry the walls shook.

"She's taking us all down together," Matt hollered.

That was crazy talk. Yes Ruben knew the figures and as Marjorie's figures had begun to dip, so had Matt's.

But that did not necessarily mean that there had to be a link, and second of all, the drop was not that bad. Nothing really serious.

That's what Ruben told Matt, first to give him the facts, and second to calm him down.

"But let me give you the facts, since you're still new around here," said Matt.

New? Really?

"I don't think you've been in the news business long enough to know what a trend looks like," Matt was saying.

"I think I do," Ruben said softly, measuring the situation and placating his own temper. "Please tell. Enlighten."

"I should apologize...I know you've been around..."

"Never mind, Matt. Go on."

Matt did not like the look in Ruben's eyes, and how calmly, too calmly he was reacting. He knew the rumors about the man.

He surely knew that Ruben came from London, plus the other rumors.

"I'm only trying to educate you about how it works in the United States."

"I appreciate being educated, Matt. Go on."

Another wrong choice of words, but there wasn't much to worry about. He'd lose a friend, but he was still top dog.

Nobody could touch him. They could talk behind his back. But they could not touch him.

"Haven't you been getting my messages?"

"Every hour on the hour, Matt. What do you want me to do?"

"Control her."

Another wrong choice of words.

"Control Marjorie Carmen. Who talks like this?"

"I brought her up, you know."

"I rather think we all did. I rather think she did most of it herself," Ruben explained, still under restraint.

"I could have gone straight upstairs about this, you know."

"I appreciate the chance."

"Figuring that you'd be the one mostly to come to terms with Marjorie," Matt said, "and what she's doing by changing the format and what we're all about."

"You mean the Poet's Corner."

"It's a loser, Ruben, and we are all losing because of it, Ruben. It's changing the brand. Haven't you noticed?"

Yes, Ruben had noticed, and he could not help but admire Marjorie for taking a step so risky.

Nobody else, anywhere in the business, had the balls to make the switch that wasn't so farfetched anyway…a 15-minute segment for intellectual reflection. Surely for those 15 minutes the tempo was down, but the quality was up. America, accustomed to trash, would get used to it, but it would take time.

That was how Ruben explained it to Matt, who said, "But people aren't getting used to it, and we're running out of time. You've seen the figures."

"They vary. We're still way ahead. We're still number one."

"My figures never vary."

"For this you blame Marjorie?"

"I blame her for trying to change the pattern that's made Alpha News so successful. This could hurt."

Yes it could, and Ruben recalled Matt going after Marjorie in other ways that could hurt, telling his audience that he couldn't figure out what she was trying to prove going highbrow, taboo this, a remark that should never be made from one anchor to another. He'd done it before and he was doing it again, but this time with more heat.

Ruben had two thoughts about bringing this up, first no, then, what the hell.

"That was a needless putdown, Matt."

Matt turned red.

"That wasn't planned."

Everything Matt did was planned.

"So you're asking someone to intervene."

"Would you?"

"You mean would I make her drop that segment?"

"Yes. For the good of the network."

"Frankly, Matt, I don't see how this is any concern of yours. She'd never ask me to intervene against you."

Not even after that "highbrow" insult of a few weeks before.

Matt started going on about his fatherly concern for Marjorie. He's the one...

"I'm sure she's very grateful to you, Matt..."

"So let her prove it," said Matt.

"Did you ask her yourself?"

"Yes, I did."

"What happened?"

* * * * *

"I told him that I resented his meddling," Marjorie was telling Ruben over drinks at Bar Six in Greenwich Village.

"That sounds mild, coming from you."

"I have to watch my back, Ruben. I can't have someone like that turning against me."

"That's not what he says."

"Okay, what does he say?"

"He says you told him to go screw himself."

"A lie. A lie, Ruben. I did tell him to go..."

"Go what?"

"Go find another patsy."

"He told me you said something else."

She laughed. "Okay, I told him to go find another pussy, besides himself."

Then she suggested a game. They should each immediately, on a secret napkin, write down two words that come to mind when describing Matt Owens.

Marjorie came up with "pompous bastard." But, with Marjorie keeping score, Ruben won with "pompous shmuck."

"I've even heard you call him a putz," she laughed.

She was beautiful when she laughed and heads did turn, although it could never be determined whether it was for her fame or beauty, or both. A few people came over for her autograph, a picture together, and quite a few stopped just to say how much they loved her and her program.

The locals were cool about it, but the out-of-towners gushed.

That's the way it usually ran and she always knew she'd have to keep a balance between hip America and down home America.

"Are you with him, Ruben?"

"Of course not."

"That's not what I mean."

"I know what you mean, and there is something to what he says. He may be a shmuck but he knows the business."

"You mean he knows numbers," she said.

"He knows ratings, yes."

"There's got to be more for us than ratings."

"What else you got?"

She stirred her drink.

"That's unfortunate," she said.

He did not want to tell her this.

"There've been complaints from affiliates."

"All of them?"

"Just a few, but enough to worry Russ."

"He brought it up?"

"He wants you to think it over."

"My Poet's Corner."

"That's what we're talking about, Marjorie."

"It's only fifteen minutes, for crying out loud."

"The word is, that it's a damper, slows everything down, stops the flow that's been the network's trademark, fast paced."

"What do you think, Ruben?"

"I think you should stick with it until you turn it around."

"Thanks," she said. "But we could both be wrong."

"I know."

"What a shame. No wonder people can't speak or think in more than 140 characters. No wonder people can't think, period. I've gotten so tired of politics and politicians and having to stay on my toes while both sides debate from prepared bullshit. It's all rehearsed. There's no impromptu anymore. Does anyone come away learning anything after two sides stop yelling at each other? I don't think so."

"I don't think so, either, Marjorie, but that's the game we play and that's the game you signed on to play."

"No, we both signed on for journalism."

"You want to bring it back to that all by yourself?"

"With your help, Ruben."

"You and me kid, right?"

"I love you, Ruben, and remember, equality is just a theory. But who's complaining?"

* * * * *

There were times when people knew it was best to stay clear of Marjorie, typically when it drew closer to show time and she'd already had her make-up done, her guest list prepared, the topics researched, and when she wanted nothing more than coffee and solitude in the cafeteria.

This day Laurie Pilgrim forgot.

"I don't mean to disturb you," said the network's managing editor.

Here goes, thought Marjorie...

"But I think you should know about the consensus around here, about your Poet's Corner."

"Oh?"

"People think it's damaging to our entire prime time schedule. I'm only telling you what they say."

"Thanks for letting me know," said Marjorie, forgetting to add the word "bitch."

"I think you need to give it some thought. Gotta run."

Give it some thought she did, and if any remark clinched it, this did. Dropping the Poet's Corner spot, or reducing it to five minutes, as some were suggesting, was now out of the question. She, Marjorie, was in with both feet and would never budge, never relent.

She had found her cause and her calling and her purpose. She would support the painter, the sculptor, the writer of poetry, the writer of prose, any of them that she believed in, and be there for them as she had never been there for her husband. This was her act of contrition.

Did the naysayers understand why she was so resolved and so fully behind her Poet's Corner? How could they be? This was personal and this was final and she would stick with it at the risk of losing everything, and even at the expense of her career and her reputation.

She owed, and she would pay. She owed it to every sin she had committed by intention or omission, and she owed it to reconcile her conscience. They would not understand this compulsion to rectify the past, and the obsession this time to get it right.

She read everything that came through, as time would allow, and became a champion for works she especially liked. She would never be dismissive or high-handed of lesser talent. She was loyal and a nurturing mother to all. If this wasn't "good television," too bad. Too damn bad.

This was her baby.

For writers who had tried but failed and were trying again, hers would be the refuge for lost causes and the home for second chances.

Poet's Corner stays.

End of discussion.

Chapter 16

"It's as simple as all that," Russ Appleton was telling Ruben in the limo that was taking Russ to the airport to catch a plane for Toledo, where the affiliates were meeting. "We lose one of them, just one, and we lose viewers, we lose advertisers, and we start paddling. That's how simple this is, but you know that already."

"I told her about that," said Ruben.

"She just won't listen. I talked to her, too. Stubborn young woman."

"Gutsy would be my word."

"Don't start that with me, Ruben. You know I'm as nuts about her as you are and gutsy, yes, but there are limits."

"If she obeyed stop signs, Russ, she wouldn't be where she is today."

"She's also in trouble, that's where she is today. You know I supported her on that writer's spot. Still do. But the people she's bringing on..."

"They're good."

"No they're not. Second raters, the lot of them."

"I'm impressed."

"Name anybody."

Ruben couldn't.

"That's what I mean," Russ growled. "She needs a Hemingway. That would perk things up. Could turn it all around."

"We have no more Hemingways, Russ."

"What about Rick Code? He's Hemingway."

"Can't get him."

"Why not?"

"He's a damned recluse."

"Never known anybody that can't be got."

Ruben had sat with kings, queens, The Queen, the Dalai Lama, and rumors that he'd had a moment with the emperor of Japan – so yes.

"She's tried, Russ."

"Not hard enough, apparently. Not hard enough to save her job, obviously."

"Huh?"

"Nothing's been decided about our girl, but I don't have the final say. For that we've got affiliates and advertisers. They run the show."

* * * * *

"Anything's possible," Iris told Rick from the hospital where her mother was undergoing surgery.

"So you don't know how long you'll be, in other words."

"She may have to move in with us for a while – would you mind?"

Reflexively he said, no, he would not mind.

"Only till she gets back on her feet."
"I understand."
"You're sure you won't mind?"
"We'll talk about it later," he said coldly. "Okay?"
Long pause.
"Okay. I guess."

* * * * *

Then there was something else, Chuck, her former husband, the Montaigne professor who suffered from suicidal tendencies.

He'd been fired, couldn't pay the rent, and needed a place to stay for the time being. Just for a few weeks, until he got back on his feet.

So would it be okay to stay with Rick and Iris?

Iris didn't have the nerve to pile this on, so she made Chuck ask Rick himself.

"Sure. Why not."

Then, a week later, Iris still with her mom, Chuck had to be rushed to the hospital after swallowing a half container of Valium.

When Iris got back with her mother, a fine woman, there were four altogether in the same house, and Iris kept eyeing Rick for signs of displeasure, but Rick kept his thoughts to himself, and besides, even if with the two of them, when there'd just been that, it wasn't the same as it had been at first.

Iris didn't have to be told and Rick didn't have to tell her. It just wasn't the same, and had stopped being the same after he'd finished the novel. Somehow she'd been part of the love affair, just by her being around and watching him type and urging him on, even if that meant bringing him a cup of coffee when she knew that it was exactly what he needed at the moment. They'd been in tune.

So that was finished, and this was finished.

He could, he thought, add rooms to the house, so that her mother could recover as she needed, and Chuck could commit suicide as often as he needed.

So he could add more rooms, or he could build a new house on the same grounds. There was plenty of room and there was plenty of money.

Or...he could pack up and go.

* * * * *

Marjorie got word from London that they'd be willing to have a chat. She'd be in no hurry.

Along with the lukewarm invitation came a strange question: Did she intend to get pregnant and have any more children?

Something like this used to baffle Russ Appleton when one of his superstars found herself in that condition and had to take a leave of absence.

"Women keep getting pregnant," he'd complain. "I don't know how this keeps happening."

After that meeting with Hiram Giddings her romance with London and a chance to be seen by the world took a turn for the worse, if they were all like that, which of course they weren't, but if she was still having trouble acting proper for a President, imagine a Queen. She'd have to learn how to curtsy. No deal.

She was an American, by God, and that was enough, and she'd go crawling to nobody.

She had a job, a job any woman would die for, and she had a responsibly as a role model, or that's how it kept being put to her. Young girls, she was told, looked up to her. She was proof, staring everyone in the face night after night through the lens at Alpha News, that feminism had arrived.

Well, that was something else, something she had no time for, the business of equality, and there were things about it all that nobody knew, like the fact that the sisterhood was not in it altogether as one, the competition being so fierce, the backstabbing so intense.

She represented no one but herself, and there were decisions to be made and as Ruben used to tell her, "Nobody tells you about the fork in the road." This was a twist she'd have to confront – over what? Over a 15-minute segment on her program that everyone, or so it seemed, wanted her to drop, which she could do upon a whim.

But there was a principle involved. She wasn't sure what is was – her respect for herself as a woman of valor, a woman who stuck by what she believed? Or was it about her being headstrong just for the sake of being ornery. Once you showed them that you could be pushed around, they pushed you around.

Once they saw you were weak, they treated you accordingly and that respect you never won back.

They'd start calling you honey and babe and expect you to get the coffee. She'd seen it happen. It was already happening to Carla Bruin, whose regular spot they now kept rotating, and once in a while compelling her to share it with a co-anchor – and that is precisely what was burning Marjorie.

Russ did not have the guts to bring it to her, so they sent Laurie Pilgrim to ask if it would be okay to have a co-anchor sit in with her.

"What?"

"We just thought it might be something for you to think about, ease your burden and all that," said Laurie, the network's managing editor.

Is this what they mean by *the writing on the wall*?

"Who's WE?"

"Management."

"Who is management?"

"Look, it's just a thought. Just a suggestion."

"Does Ruben know about this?"

"Actually, no."

"That's my answer. Actually no. No!"

"There's no need to take it out on me, Marjorie. I'm just the messenger."

Marjorie never did like her, feelings were mutual from day one. In fact Marjorie doubted that even Russ had anything to do with this.

Sounded like an operation coming strictly from Laurie Pilgrim. Sounded like the handiwork of a sister from the sisterhood, one role model to another.

* * * * *

Ruben had ways. The old boy network was still at his disposal. Not for nothing had he been a member of the Mossad, or something like the Mossad, and using the tricks of the trade, managed to track down the most famous writer in the world, and the most reclusive, Rick Code.

He had men he trusted reach the compound. Ruben never knew the details when such sleuthing was done, and he never wanted to know, just so long as the job was done. But he wanted more than an address. He wanted the means to speak with this reclusive author, and this too they delivered.

Ruben made the call and Rick picked up and Ruben did not know that this was Marjorie's good old husband, only that this was the great writer that everyone pursued, to no avail. But could he make one exception. Ruben expected the click.

But the man at the other end of the line, whose voice Ruben did not recognize, it sounded alcoholic and gravelly from smoking, responded.

He asked what this was all about. Ruben explained the situation.

"I'll think about it," was what he said, and hung up.

Chapter 17

Rick Code took his walk within the woods and around the neighborhood, thinking it over. He did not see it as a drama that had come full circle.

He saw it as an enigma, the one where we scheme and dream and God laughs.

He was not pleased that Ruben had to come groveling to him for Marjorie's sake. He liked Ruben, despite everything.

So it gave him no delight and no thrill to find Ruben so humiliated. Well we all get a turn, and he recalled his own humiliation at that gala, and how he'd got even with that man, that evil man, the lawyer, the lawyer for the studio, and how even that had solved nothing – except to bring down a billion dollar movie.

Humiliation is good, Rick was thinking. It's payment for something we did or were prepared to do. Someone is settling a score.

That's a religious belief and Rick was not religious, but something had happened to him.

He did not feel religious about Matt Owens because he knew that it was Matt Owens who was out to get Marjorie, and he knew why, the envy, the obnoxious superiority, for starters, and Rick could picture it all, but it did not require much of an imagination to figure it out, that the son of a bitch was on the warpath to put her in her place.

He'd need help, and he'd get it from Russ Appleton and surely from Laurie Pilgrim, but not from Ruben, no, not Ruben, but Russ would be enough.

Save for Ruben, she never really did have friends there, not really, nobody really, nobody true, and that is why he was never really as jealous about it as a husband ought to be, and the time had come to bring out that cliché about those chickens coming home to roost.

He could tell that she was hurting and it was no secret, not to Rick, that they'd found her Poet's Corner as the weapon to take her down.

He knew it wasn't working. He was bored himself, and if he was bored what about the rest of the country that only read cookbooks and books about how to lose weight. Serious talk wasn't catchy, nobody was dancing with these stars, and these writers, these writers she was featuring night after night were not exactly Dick Cavett, Truman Capote or Norman Mailer.

They were lightweights with the usual one book a year they were forced to produce for their publishers, whether they had anything to say or not.

They had nothing to say, to be honest, but Marjorie would persist. He knew Marjorie. Once she got something into her head, she wouldn't let go.

That was Marjorie all right.

But the strain was showing. He knew the fake laugh and the fake ebullience. She was still fooling the rest of the country, but not him.

He knew a collapse was coming. Only a matter of time.

* * * * *

He continued his walk and he'd come to enjoy that part of the day when he'd stroll the neighborhood at the time when the kids were coming home from school, and waved to him. He waved back. He was not the strange man anymore. He'd been invited to the school to give a talk. They knew who he was, the great author, but kept it to themselves, as he'd asked them to do.

He gave a short talk, though mostly he answered questions. He wanted to know if they were worried about the future and the question was odd to them, as at that age they did not worry about the future because they did not know what a future was. So they weren't worried about it, and none of them talked about wanting to be firemen, cowboys or athletes as it had been in his day.

These days they wanted to be rich. They wanted to make it through technology. They knew the terms better than he did.

"Doesn't anybody want to be a writer like our honored guest?" asked the teacher.

Many raised their arms.

"Would you be kind enough to teach them some rules?" the teacher asked Rick Code.

He offered the usual rule, the one that worked for himself – "Write your heart out, and then cut it in half."

He then added that if they did not understand what he meant by that today, they would understand it later on.

But he only spoke once to the class, and this was only because reporters from the local newspaper started coming around.

This spooked him.

Later in fact an item about his visiting the class appeared in the *Herald*, which was one thing, but when it got picked up by the wires and the *Times*, that was something else, and when people wondered if Rick Code was coming out of his shell – if indeed that was Rick Code, he'd had enough.

So he'd never do that again.

But he still enjoyed his daily walks, and this time he had Marjorie Carmen on his mind as it concerned her very own future. She was no schoolgirl, though apparently the big boys were beginning to treat her like one, forgetting that as she had grown up around Alpha News, Alpha News had grown up around her.

She was as responsible as anyone, even Matt Owens, for the network's success, a success in doubt from day one, since nobody knew if it would work, round the clock news, which worked on radio, but for television that sort of format still needed to be tested.

She deserved better, Rick was thinking, and somebody needs to wake up to realize what they'd be losing if they lost her.

She'd only take so much before she'd decide to bolt. She had other offers, only, he was thinking, this may not be the best time to start tinkering, since the industry knew what was going on, that her numbers were staying flat if not decreasing, she was on the outs with Russ Appleton for being so stubborn about her Poet's Corner, and altogether there was murmuring among the staff and along the grapevine – and, she was nearing 40.

The timing would be wrong to make a move.

Where do they go after they reach 40? With men it's different, it is different, he had to admit, though he was no feminist, or whatever it was, or how different it was today from the day when it got started, when a woman giving the news or offering commentary would cause America to laugh.

Well that joke is over and done through women like Marjorie Carmen, and the others.

So what happens? He could not imagine her settled into a life of domesticity. Marjorie needed the action.

Marjorie needed the juice. Could she switch and become an actress? No, those people had scripts that would take years to develop.

Marjorie needed on the spot action. She could not be made to sit still and be patient.

She'd never make it as a writer. That too took time. She'd thought about it when they were together.

But then she'd be in competition with her husband, Rick Callow, when it was Rick she was trying to uplift.

He realized that now, that she had done her best, the fault was his and his alone, and on this day he made a decision.

* * * * *

On the same day, Ruben Franklin sat in his office preparing to meet Russ at the airport. Russ had phoned that they needed to talk right away. Details to follow. This concerned him. Something was up. Well it was always something in this business and in life, but this seemed to be something special – and not in a good way.

But he had a few moments to check the latest news online, always, first, to check out the competition and who if anyone was beating them to the punch, because there was still that from the old days, when newspapers killed, actually killed to be first with the news, and it still was like that today, except that the news moved much faster.

Back then news moved by the calendar. These days it moved by the clock and there was never such a thing as being all caught up.

You were always behind and if you stayed behind too long, you were in the wrong business. People didn't know this, but delivering the news was like any type of selling and salesmanship, and if your merchandise got stale you were Willy Loman and we know what happened to him.

What could it be?

But that was one of Russ Appleton's most famous tricks, to say we need to talk...but later...to keep you on edge...and worrying enough to drive you crazy.

Ruben never worried, but the others did, whenever that routine came up?

What does he want? What does it mean? Is my job on the line? That's how it was in this business, or in any business, everybody so insecure.

Nothing like that for Ruben, and who was that man who said, it is good to be rich? So true. For Ruben, absolutely true.

He could buy the network and still have plenty left.

But something was up, if not for him, then for people he liked, one that he loved, so Ruben allowed himself a trace of concern.

Then he smiled reading something quite expected online, and it was an item running short and unimportant, saying that in the case of a murdered motel operator, named Leroy Larson, one of his sons, Clyde, was being charged with manslaughter. The piece continued to say that murder one was being ruled out because there was evidence of a fight to the death between father and son, so no malice aforethought.

Moreover, there'd been bad blood within the entire family. Neighbors testified to this, adding that the father had been a brute.

He was known to put the birch to his sons for no good reason, so what happened was no surprise.

The man deserved to die, yes he did, thought Ruben, but for other reasons, a reason known only to him, and to Marjorie.

She was very worried at first, but stopped being worried when he assured her that he was taking care of the business.

Apparently, according to rumor, the son had confessed. There was another rumor that he had taken a million dollars to take the rap.

The investigation continues.

Chapter 18

"No, I'm not calling it a disaster," Russ was telling Ruben riding in the limo from the airport to the newsroom.

Russ was back from his meeting with the affiliates.

"But I am calling it an uprising."

"So I gathered," said Ruben.

"Well gather this. If your girl Marjorie doesn't shape up..."

Now she was his girl, not Russ Appleton's girl.

"If she doesn't come to her senses, and fast, we could all be in trouble."

"But we're not being dropped."

"There is that threat," Russ said, "from a few, but when that starts..."

"I understand."

"Do you?"

"What do they want?"

"You won't believe this," said Russ.

"Try me."

"Matt Owens has been lobbying against her behind our backs. Not that they needed him to tell them what's been going on with her Poet's Corner."

"I'll have a talk with Matt."

"I know you will. But be careful. Can't lose him."

"But we can lose Marjorie, Russ? Marjorie?"

"I hear you, Ruben. But that spot is killing the works. Have you talked to her, I mean again?"

"Yes, I have," said Ruben.

"Still stubborn?"

"Russ, I've taken her side."

"You too? I have to fight both of you? You don't get it, do you?"

"The spot needs time. Damn it, give her the time."

"I'm not your worry, Ruben. It's the affiliates."

"Precisely what do they want?"

"Precisely they want it dropped, or..."

"Or..."

Russ stopped to collect his thoughts.

"Well there's one last chance."

"Well that's something."

"Not much," said Russ. "But if she can start replacing those dunces with somebody big to liven things up, the pressure would be off."

"They're not dunces, Russ."

"They're nobodies. She needs a big name to turn it all around."

"We've discussed this before," said Ruben.

"That's right. She needs Hemingway."

"Which we agreed, was Rick Code."

"Right. Literary star power, and then others along that level would jump right in. It would be a much different show. So?"

"Okay, yes...I have reached out to him," said Ruben.

"Still a recluse?"

"I've talked to him."

"I thought he talks to nobody."

"We spoke."

"I figured if anybody...and?"

"There's a chance. There's a chance we could get him."

"How big of a chance, Ruben?"

"I don't know."

"When will we know?"

"Monday."

"Monday when?"

"Morning."

"He's in town?"

"I'm not sure."

"Is he supposed to meet with you?"

"No. He's supposed to meet with her."

"You think he'll do that, Ruben?"

"I don't know, Russ."

"You think he'll show?"

"Anything's possible," said Ruben.

CPSIA information can be obtained
at www.ICGtesting.com
Printed in the USA
BVOW08s2151011116
466666BV00001B/2/P